PRAISE FOR THE JACK S

THRESHOLD

"In Robinson's latest action fest, Jack Sigler, King of the Chess Team--a Delta Forces unit whose gonzo members take the names of chess pieces--tackles his most harrowing mission yet. Threshold elevates Robinson to the highest tier of over-the-top action authors and it delivers beyond the expectations even of his fans. The next Chess Team adventure cannot come fast enough."-- **Booklist - Starred Review**

"In Robinson's wildly inventive third Chess Team adventure (after Instinct), the U.S. president, Tom Duncan, joins the team in mortal combat against an unlikely but irresistible gang of enemies, including "regenerating capybara, Hydras, Neander-thals, [and] giant rock monsters." ...Video game on a page? Absolutely. Fast, furious unabashed fun? You bet." -- **Publishers Weekly**

"Jeremy Robinson's *Threshold* is one hell of a thriller, wildly imaginative and diabolical, which combines ancient legends and modern science into a non-stop action ride that will keep you turning the pages until the wee hours. Relentlessly gripping from start to finish, don't turn your back on this book!"
-- **Douglas Preston, New York Times bestselling author of Impact and Blasphemy**

"With *Threshold* Jeremy Robinson goes pedal to the metal into very dark territory. Fast-paced, action-packed and wonderfully creepy! Highly recommended!" -- **Jonathan Maberry, *New York Times* bestselling author of *The King of Plagues* and *Rot & Ruin***

"*Threshold* is a blisteringly original tale that blends the thriller and horror genres in a smooth and satisfying hybrid mix. With his new entry in the Jack Sigler series, Jeremy Robinson plants his feet firmly on territory blazed by David Morrell and James Rollins. The perfect blend of mysticism and monsters, both human and otherwise, make *Threshold* as groundbreaking as it is riveting." -- **Jon Land,** *New York Times* **bestselling author** of *Strong Enough to Die*

"Jeremy Robinson is the next James Rollins."-- **Chris Kuzneski, New York Times bestselling author of The Lost Throne and The Prophecy**

"Jeremy Robinson's *Threshold* sets a blistering pace from the very first page and never lets up. This globe-trotting thrill ride challenges its well-crafted heroes with ancient mysteries, fantastic creatures, and epic action sequences. For readers seeking a fun rip-roaring adventure, look no further."
 -- **Boyd Morrison, bestselling author of** *The Ark*

"Robinson artfully weaves the modern day military with ancient history like no one else."-- **Dead Robot Society**

"THRESHOLD is absolutely gripping. A truly unique story mixed in with creatures and legendary figures of mythology, technology and more fast-paced action than a Jerry Bruckheimer movie. If you want fast-paced: you got it. If you want action: you got it. If you want mystery: you got it, and if you want intrigue, well, you get the idea. In short, I $@#!$% loved this one."-- **thenovelblog.com**

"As always the Chess Team is over the top of the stratosphere, but anyone who relishes an action urban fantasy thriller that combines science and mythology will want to join them for the exhilarating Pulse pumping ride."-- **Genre Go Round Reviews**

CALLSIGN:

KNIGHT

JEREMY ROBINSON

WITH ETHAN CROSS

BREAKNECK MEDIA

Visit Jeremy Robinson on the World Wide Web at:
 www.jeremyrobinsononline.com

Visit Ethan Cross on the World Wide Web at:
www.ethancross.com

FICTION BY JEREMY ROBINSON

The Antarktos Saga
The Last Hunter - Pursuit
The Last Hunter - Descent

The Jack Sigler Thrillers
Threshold
Instinct
Pulse
Callsign: King - Book 1
Callsign: Queen - Book 1
Callsign: Rook - Book 1
Callsign: Bishop - Book 1
Callsign: Knight - Book 1
Callsign: King - Book 2 - Underworld

Origins Editions (first five novels)
Kronos
Antarktos Rising
Beneath
Raising the Past
The Didymus Contingency

Writing as Jeremy Bishop
Torment
The Sentinel

Short Stories
Insomnia

Humor
The Zombie's Way (Ike Onsoomyu)
The Ninja's Path (Kutyuso Deep)

FICTION BY ETHAN CROSS

The Shepherd
The Cage

CALLSIGN:

KNIGHT

1.

Shin Dae-jung—Callsign: Knight, could detect most attacks before they struck. What his keen ears and eyes didn't detect, he could normally feel, as though he possessed some kind of sixth sense. Most soldiers experienced this from time to time, but Knight, as a member of the ultra-black ops Chess Team, relied on it more than most. So when he felt a tingling on his skin, he tensed and filled his lungs to shout a warning, but the pilot, Captain Daniel Mueller, beat him to the punch. "Instrumentation is down!" Mueller shouted.

"We're going down!" called the co-pilot, whose name Knight never learned.

Knight's training didn't allow him to panic. He quickly analyzed the situation to determine if there was anything that he could do to help. Unfortunately, double-checking his seatbelt and gripping his armrests were his only options.

The transport was a hybrid aircraft known as a CV-22B Osprey that combined the hovering and vertical take-off and landing abilities of a helicopter and the long-range transport capabilities and speed of an airplane. It had wings like a plane but also had four prop-rotors powered by turboprop engines, and transmission nacelles mounted on each wingtip that could tilt up or down. It had been painted black for use by special ops. Knight supposed that if he was going die in a crash, at least he was doing it in style.

"I'm going to try and sit it down on top of one of these buildings," Mueller said. "Hang on!"

Knight tried to focus his mind on his surroundings instead of his impending death. The sound in the cabin wasn't as he expected however. It was eerily quiet. In other crashes he had experienced, a million different noises compounded upon each other and created a deafening wall of sound. Blaring alarms, flashing lights, the squealing of a broken rotor blade or damaged engine, the sound of enemy fire still rattling against the chopper's fuselage, the buckling of metal, the roar and snap of fire. He wondered for a moment why everything was so quiet. Then, he realized what had hit them. It could only have been some type of electro-magnetic pulse weapon, a device designed to overload electronic systems, which meant that the Osprey had been converted into a twenty-ton glider.

He opened his eyes but immediately regretted doing so. The large gray concrete walls of a parking garage loomed ahead, and he knew from experience that they were coming in much too fast for a safe landing.

He braced himself as the belly of the Osprey struck the surface of the parking garage and skidded forward. Sparks shot up from the friction on the concrete from the bird's metal belly.

Mueller tried to direct the Osprey sideways and away from the approaching sidewall of the structure. But they were moving too fast, and he had too little control. The Osprey burst through the wall, sending fragments of concrete raining down, and careened forward over the edge of the building.

Knight's stomach climbed into his throat as the ground fell out from beneath them and they plummeted downward. He fought the urge to tighten his muscles for the impact, knowing that being relaxed and loose during a crash could save your life.

This was the reason that so many drunk drivers survived a crash while their victims were killed.

Luckily, the parking structure had a multi-tiered design, and they only had three levels to fall. The nose of the Osprey struck the concrete and dug a groove as its momentum pushed it forward. The contents of the cabin tore free from the harnesses, and a large supply box slammed against Knight's side. The smell of charred metal and hydraulic fluids filled the air, and the screeching of metal on metal sounded like a freight train throwing on its brakes. The Osprey slid sideways to the middle of the empty parking garage's roof and then finally came to a stop.

He didn't waste any time. He popped off his restraints and stepped over the scattered mess of the cabin toward the cockpit. Mueller was conscious, but his leg had been trapped when the Osprey's nose had compacted. The co-pilot, on the other hand, was very dead—his chest impaled by wreckage.

Damnit, Knight thought, but stopped himself from thinking about the dead man. They'd been attacked. He was sure. That meant time was short. Knight positioned himself on Mueller's side and grabbed hold of the control panel pressing against the man's leg. "Okay, I'm going to try and push this up. You pull your leg free."

Mueller's head bobbed up and down rapidly.

"One…two…three." He pressed up on the panel with all his strength. Mueller cried out and pulled himself away. Some of the metal had pierced the man's left leg, but with a scream of pain, he tore it free, widening the gash.

Knight dropped the panel and moved to Mueller's side. He glanced at the wound on the man's leg and sighed. Knight reached to his belt—a fifteen hundred dollar stingray skin belt—and unbuckled it. He wrapped the belt around the man's leg and cinched it tight, coating the pricey accoutrement in blood. He could afford another one—his parents had been

wealthy, leaving their small fortune to him when they died—
but he didn't like seeing nice clothing ruined. He lived simply
most of the time, especially while on base or on a mission. But
he dressed to the nines and traveled to exotic locations—and
women—when he could, which is exactly what he had been
doing before his vacation had been cut short in the middle of a
date with a pretty blonde he'd met at the beach.

Unfortunately, when he had been pulled into this mission,
he hadn't been given any details. He was told that he would
receive a briefing and all of the necessary equipment when he
arrived. He hadn't even been given time to change his clothes,
and he still wore his eight thousand dollar Brioni cream silk suit
and printed silk shirt.

With the bleeding contained, he pulled Mueller from the
wreckage and propped him against the far wall of the parking
structure. "Sit tight. I'm going to grab some supplies."

He climbed back into the downed Osprey's cabin and
searched the mess for anything that they might need. He assumed that they were close to the rendezvous point, but they
were also in hostile territory. He needed weapons.

The back half of the cabin contained a four-wheel ATV
that he assumed would have been for his use on the mission. It
was black with a supply rack mounted on the back containing
extra fuel and spots for storing weapons and ammo. He noticed
a bulletproof shield mounted to the handlebars and nitrous
oxide boosters connected to the engine. He could have had
some fun with it, but it was useless now. The EMP would have
fried it as it had the Osprey, and the bay doors were wedged
shut.

Next to the ATV, he found the weapons locker. It was
locked tight, but he found a piece of metal that had torn free
from the fuselage and was able to use leverage to snap the lock
free. The locker contained a row of standard issue M4 carbine
assault rifles, but the last in line had been modified with a

grenade launcher. He grabbed it, two Beretta 9mm handguns and some extra ammunition.

He returned to Mueller, snapped a magazine into the M4, jacked back the slide and then looked out over the ghost city. From his vantage point, he could see a good distance in both directions. The cityscape resembled any other modern metropolis with skyscrapers, traffic lights, shopping malls, parking garages, store fronts, subways and office buildings. The difference here was that this city—called Shenhuang—lacked a major component possessed by all the other cities of the world. It was empty. No one lived there.

The Chinese government had built sprawling urban centers like Shenhuang in remote areas of their country to raise their gross national product and make their country appear as if it were sustaining growth. In actuality, the Chinese people couldn't afford to live within the new cities with estimates putting the number of empty homes at as many as sixty four million. But the government had no plans of stopping their expansion as they continued to build twenty new cities every year within China's vast areas of open country.

Normally, the few people who did live in the cities were maintenance workers and government authorities. This particular city, however, had been evacuated. The government claimed that it was due to a chemical spill, but Knight suspected it was to a far more nefarious end. The evacuation of a city that hardly anyone lived in, however, hadn't been enough to draw much international scrutiny.

The wind blew up from the streets and ruffled his dark, black hair. It blew the smells of the crash from his mind. The air smelled clean and cool. No hint of the pollution or car exhaust that he had become accustomed to in other cities. The air smelled like country air, but not quite. It was missing something. In the countryside, the smells of flowers, crops and vegetation permeated every breath. But the air here was oddly sterile.

The one nice thing about the city being uninhabited was that he would be able to spot their enemy coming from a mile away. But as his eyes passed over the towers of glass and concrete and the roads labeled in Chinese script, he couldn't see a single person, enemy or otherwise.

"Can you move?" he said to Mueller.

"I think my leg's broken, but I'll make it."

Knight slid an arm under Mueller's shoulders and lifted him from the pavement. The pilot stood six inches taller than Knight, which made carrying him down the stairs of the parking garage a formidable task. But within a few moments, they had reached the bottom floor and set off down the empty street of the ghost city.

2.

The creature watched the two small things pull themselves from the wreckage of the metal bird. It didn't hate them, but knew it would soon taste their blood. And killing them would be easy. The small things were so fragile and afraid. They would scream and run, and fire their weapons, but the creature felt no fear. They could not harm it, though a part of it longed for death.

The beast stretched out a clawed hand and scratched its razor-sharp talons against its concrete perch. An image from the past entered its mind from another life. Something called a gargoyle. They hung menacingly on the sides of buildings. But it wasn't a gargoyle, at least it didn't think so. It wasn't actually sure what it was.

The small device attached to its ear beeped to life and the master's voice filled its mind. "Huangdi, I want you to kill the two soldiers, but I want you to do so quietly and slowly. Play with them a bit. Give us a show."

The creature looked to the two fragile things. When the master commanded, it had to answer. That was what it had been programmed to do. It thought of the screams of the other small things, and some strange feeling overwhelmed it. Its mind fought to put a name to the emotion. Regret? Shame? It knew the words but couldn't associate a meaning.

It didn't think that it enjoyed the killing, but its mind was so clouded and confused that it couldn't tell one way or the other. The only thing that brought clarity, certainty and understanding was the objective. It was the only graspable thread, the only connection to the world it had lost.

The objective brought peace.

And right now, the objective was to kill the two small things.

3.

Knight sensed that they were being watched. That animal part of his brain that had saved him so many times in the past screamed that they were not alone. He learned to trust his instincts long ago, but his options were limited.

Mueller was a dead weight against his shoulder, and his lungs burned for air from carrying the man down the ten flights of stairs necessary to reach street level. He dropped the wounded soldier onto the curb and glanced around the abandoned streets.

The buildings were beautiful and clean—shining pillars of glass, concrete and steel that would have been at home in any major city within the U.S.. The only difference being that these buildings were empty, while scores of men, women and children inhabited their U.S. counterparts. In fact, Knight was sure that this was the cleanest street he had ever seen, much cleaner than even the most environmentally conscious city back in the states.

Empty storefronts and lobbies decorated with red and white realtor signs coupled with the lack of cars and people gave rise to memories of the best visions of the apocalypse that Hollywood had churned out. But in most of those films, the buildings and streets were in decay and falling in on themselves.

The cleanliness and beauty of the scene actually made it feel more disturbing, as if all the people in the world had simply vanished.

Knight turned back to Mueller and said, "Where's the rendezvous point?"

Mueller coughed into his hand. He was tall with sandy blonde hair and a surfer's tan, but his voice sounded small and frail. "Judging from our last position before we went down, we're a little over three clicks from the staging area. We were supposed to land in the parking lot outside of an empty warehouse in the industrial district. I don't know what the hell hit us."

Knight's eyes continued to scan the buildings as he replied. "Most people don't get to feel an electromagnetic pulse. They're most commonly associated as an after effect of a nuclear detonation. But the eggheads have also been developing directed EMP weaponry for years. Which means that whoever hit us is well-equipped."

He squatted down to eye level with Mueller and fixed him with an intense gaze. "If you know anything about this mission, you need to tell me right now."

Mueller shrugged. "Sorry, the brass never tells me anything. They just say where and when to fly, and that's what I do. I don't ask questions, and I figure that if I need to know, then somebody'll fill me in."

"Well, I need to know. You're sure that you didn't hear anything?"

Mueller hesitated a moment and then said, "I did hear a rumor about a covert military base being hit and a whole team of spec ops soldiers being wiped out, but I figured it was just a ghost story."

Knight shook his head and cursed General Keasling for dragging him into this mess without even supplying him with the basic details of the mission. He had been wreck diving off the coast of Thailand for the week, and had been enjoying good food and beautiful company, when he had received the message. Deep Blue, a.k.a. Tom Duncan, the former president of the United States, and the brains behind Chess Team, informed him that Keasling had requested the team's brand of assistance on a very sensitive black op into China. Keasling had provided a time and location for pickup and little else. Knight had been instructed to rendezvous with a team from Delta already onsite where he would receive a full briefing and equipment. He shook his head in disgust; there was nothing like jumping blind into a hot zone. It was never supposed to play out that way in the age of information, but Keasling always did play his cards close to the chest.

Movement within one of the nearby windows drew his attention, and he instantly sighted the M4 in on the spot. Scanning for further signs of life, he scooped up Mueller and moved him to a more protected location within a nearby alley. He expected the narrow alleyway to be dotted by overflowing garbage cans, dumpsters and stray cats, but it was completely empty from end to end.

He pulled out one of the Berettas he had retrieved from the Osprey's wreckage, chambered a round and handed it to Mueller. "Sit tight and watch your back. I'm going to find out who knocked us out of the sky."

Moving silently, Knight moved inside the building, M4 raised, finger on the trigger. He used the pressure switch beneath his thumb to activate the flashlight on the end of the M4. The narrow beam of illumination paused on a sign that read Department of Urban Development and Control. He guessed that this was some type of government building. The reception desk was bare and covered by a thin layer of dust.

Backtracking the movement he had seen, he moved down a large windowless hallway with doors on both sides. Most of the doors stood open to vacant offices, but the final door on the right led into a room filled with a few modest cubicles. Only a few of the desks sported office supplies and family portraits, but it was still somewhat comforting to find even the smallest sign of life.

He moved toward a bank of windows on the far wall and peered out. He could see the spot on the street where he had been standing just moments before. This was the right window, but where was the watcher?

4.

Mueller examined a wound on his shoulder and adjusted the tourniquet that Knight had applied to his leg. He winced as tendrils of pain lanced through the limb. He pressed his head against the concrete wall at his back and tried to rise above the pain. The lesion on his leg went down to the bone and he knew that if he didn't receive true medical attention soon, he would die from infection and blood loss.

His thoughts turned to his family back home. His younger brother had been the varsity quarterback that year, and he'd never even seen him play. His little sister was a freshman in college, and he had missed her high school graduation. He thought of his mother's special white chicken chili, which only served to remind him of the last time he had visited and the argument with his father. Now, bleeding to death thousands of miles from home, he wished that he would have lived his life differently. He didn't regret his service or being away. But he did regret the choices he had made when he was home and the unimportant things that had taken priority over his family.

A rustling down the street drew him back to the moment, and he raised his pistol in that direction. He considered calling out Knight's name, but he resisted the urge. If it was Knight, he would know soon enough. He could tell the well-dressed man was some kind of specials ops operator. The way he carried himself—the confidence—meant the man had seen some crazy action and come out with his good looks intact. Believing Knight, whose real name was a mystery, was the cream of the U.S. crop gave him hope. Then again, it might not be Knight making noise. In fact, it seemed unlikely. The man moved like a ghost. And if it wasn't Knight...

He felt a throbbing in his wounds as his heart pumped hard and surged extra blood through his veins. He had seldom been in combat outside of the cockpit, but he had been in this situation enough to recognize the distinct feeling of being watched by enemy eyes.

Dust rained down onto his head and shoulders, and he heard a scratching sound coming from above him.

The breath caught in his throat, but he forced himself into action. His muscles tensed, and he whipped the pistol up, expecting to see an enemy descending upon him.

But there was nothing there.

He pointed the gun back down the street, the sensation of being watched still a thorn in his mind.

5.

Knight caught movement out of the corner of his eye and jerked the M4 back in that direction. Two dark figures moved swiftly toward the door.

He didn't hesitate.

He sprinted back toward the cubicles. The first row of office spaces had a low barrier and a flat shelf instead of a high walled enclosure. Upon reaching these first cubicles, he threw his shoulder down and rolled over the top of the barrier.

He didn't miss a beat as he hit the ground running and took off after the fleeing watchers. His prey were weaving in and out of the rows, trying to reach the far door.

Knight realized that he wasn't going to catch them before they reached the exit. Deciding upon a different tactic, he turned a corner and grabbed a rolling office chair sitting against one of the desks. He raised his leg, pressing his foot squarely against the seat of the chair. Then, he kicked the chair toward the two fleeing figures.

The chair rolled down the aisle and collided with the smaller of the two. A tiny, frail voice cried out, and the small form careened over one of the desks.

Knight closed the distance between them and grabbed the

small Asian boy by the arm. The boy's companion, an older girl of no more than fourteen, screamed at him and lashed out with a flurry of punches and kicks.

Knight kept her at bay with his free arm. "Hey, hey. It's okay. Calm down!"

Eventually, the girl backed away and looked up at him with a smooth tear-streaked face. She was a beautiful girl with a small, upturned nose and long raven-black hair. Her clothes were expensive brands but were dirty and torn. He could smell the stench of body odor emanating from the pair and pegged them as some kind of homeless street kids. Their kind wasn't uncommon in any major metropolitan area, but to his knowledge, these ghost cities were largely uninhabited and shouldn't have any problems with the homeless, especially kids.

"Please don't hurt us. We're sorry that we were watching you," the girl said in Mandarin.

He released his grip on the boy, and the child quickly slipped behind the older girl, squeezing onto her leg. Each member of Knight's black ops Special Forces team, known as Chess Team, had each learned a variety of languages for the different regions of the world based on their heritage. Since Knight was of Korean descent, he knew nearly all of the Asiatic languages. In a soothing and confident tone, he responded back to the girl in her native tongue. "It's okay. I'm not going to hurt you. I'm a friend."

The girl didn't seem convinced. He slid the M4 to the side. He would have bent down to her level, but the girl wasn't much shorter than him. He guessed she was around fourteen years old; the boy, maybe nine. Instead, he perched on the edge of one of the desks and relaxed his posture to make himself seem less threatening.

"My name is Knight. What's yours?"

She shied back a bit, her shoulders shrinking up and her eyes darting around the room as if she was searching for an exit, but eventually she said, "My name is Ling, and this is my brother Wu Jiao. But everyone calls him Jiao."

He smiled. "Pleasure to meet you both. What are you doing here in the city by yourselves? Everyone was supposed to have been evacuated."

Ling's face scrunched up as if she had detected a bad odor. "My uncle was one of the city's maintenance workers. Our parents were killed last year so we moved here to be with uncle. He's...an unkind man and *two* kids..."

Knight understood what she was saying. The fines and extra taxes for having more than one child would have been inherited by the uncle who took them in. While taking them in might have been a mercy, it seemed his compassion had run out with his cash flow.

"We ran away. There are lots of places to hide in this city, if you can find food. We were on our own when the evacuation order was given."

He didn't press her on the relationship with her uncle. The abuse she had suffered was written all over her face. "Okay, guys. You're okay now. I'm going to be meeting up with some friends shortly, and we'll find a safe place for you. Just follow me."

He moved down the hallway toward the exit, but the children didn't follow. He turned the flashlight back on them. "Let's go. Beat your feet."

The little boy trembled in the beam of light. He shook his head from side to side and started to sob.

"What's wrong?"

The little boy mumbled something that Knight couldn't understand. He could only pick out one of the words among the boy's frightened ramble.

Monster.

6.

The boy's words shook Knight to the core. While some adults would attribute the child's claims to an overactive imagination, he knew that there were monsters in the world. He had seen them with his own eyes. He had fought them, and he had the scars to prove it. But unfortunately, the cruelest monsters he had ever faced were men of flesh and blood. Men like Richard Ridley, the former head of Manifold Genetics. Men like Ling's uncle.

He squatted down to the boy's level. "Don't worry, kid. I'm a monster hunter."

The boy's eyes perked up. "Really?"

"That's right. Stick with me, and you'll be just fine. I promise."

A string of gunfire drew his attention away from the boy. He swore under his breath and headed toward the building's entrance. The children reluctantly followed. He checked the street through the M4's ACOG scope. He didn't see any movement or anything suspicious, so he called the children after him, and they went to check on Mueller.

He kept a cautious eye out as they rounded the corner, but he wasn't prepared for what he saw. Mueller was gone. In the spot where Knight had left the man, was a scattering of spent 9mm shell casings and a pool of blood.

He heard a gasp behind him, and he grabbed for Jiao as the boy ran back out of the alley. The boy made it into the middle of the road before Knight could catch him. When he finally reached the child, he said, "We stay together, kid. No running off. Okay?"

The boy nodded, and Knight said, "You were right. Let's get back inside."

A shadow overhead blocked out the sun.

Knight's reaction was instantaneous. He rolled to the side, holding Jiao under his arm. His free hand shot out and grabbed Ling by the shoulder, pulling her along with him.

In the spot where they had just stood, a massive chunk of concrete struck the pavement, splintering the road and sending a cloud of cement dust and rock chips into the air. He didn't waste any time trying to determine the origin of the attack. Whatever had been large enough to toss a chunk of concrete the size of a Mini-Cooper wasn't an enemy that he wanted to face with only an M4 and two kids in tow.

As he pulled the children toward the building's entrance, he heard a sound that he had hoped to never hear again. The high-pitched, rattling wail that filled the streets at his back, echoing off sidewalks and the glass of empty office buildings, was eerily similar to that of a beast that he had thought long dead. A creature that had regenerative abilities the likes of which the modern world had never seen. A monster of legend that Chess Team had found was actually based upon fact. The Hydra.

7.

Knight slammed the door behind them and pushed the children into the building. The boy tripped over his own feet, but Knight was there to catch him and drive them forward. The roaring at his back grew louder. Closer.

"There's a bomb shelter in the basement," Ling said.

"Show me. Quick."

Ling bolted off toward a large, gray door marked by the symbol for stairs. Knight scooped the boy up and threw his small frame over one shoulder like a fireman escaping a burning building.

Ling reached the stairwell door first and held it for the others. Knight slammed it shut behind them. "Move!" he said, urging her into the bowels of the structure.

Above, he heard the screech of glass and metal tearing apart. Whatever was out there was small enough to follow them inside but large enough to destroy half the structure while doing it. He thought of the first time he had faced the Hydra inside one of Manifold Genetics's *Alpha* facility in New Hampshire— the subterranean complex that would soon become Chess Team's clandestine base of operations. He could still hear the screams of the researchers and security personnel when the beast awakened from its several thousand-year slumber and attacked. The sound of thundering footsteps from the floor above and the memory of screams pushed his legs to churn faster.

When they hit the door to the floor below, Ling pushed inside and pointed down the corridor. "We're almost there. Follow me!"

She shot off down the hallway, and he was on her heels. He had been trained to quickly notice the details of his surroundings. It was a skill that had saved his life on many occasions. In this hallway, he immediately recognized vacant security stations and signs reading *Authorized Personnel Only*.

Ling pushed through an open door that adjoined one of the security stations. The door was clear, but he could tell that it was made of bullet and impact resistant Lexan polycarbonate. They ran into a long concrete maintenance tunnel lit by bare bulbs hanging from a conduit along the ceiling. The air was stale.

A loud banging noise echoed out from the stairwell, and he guessed that their pursuer had just burst through the door to the floor above and would be upon them within a moment. He slammed the security door shut and hoped that it had some sort of automatic locking mechanism.

"This way!" Ling said.

A large hatch resembling that of a bank vault loomed ahead. He could hear the thing coming down the stairs, but he didn't risk looking back.

Ling ran forward in front of him down the long concrete tunnel. She glanced back over her shoulder and lost her balance. She stumbled forward and slid to the ground.

Knight scooped her up as he passed, carrying her the rest of the way. They reached the hatch, and he slid inside, dropping the children to a white tile floor.

His eyes shot back to the wall next to the hatch, searching for some mechanism to close the massive steel door. He found a red button along the right edge of the opening and pressed it. The sound of grinding gears gave him some solace, but the closing mechanism hadn't been designed for speed.

He heard the security door burst inward. The resistant material the door was made from provided little protection against a force that could break it free from its frame.

The creature's size was substantial enough that it could barely fit its bulk into the large tunnel. Knight still couldn't catch a clear view of the thing. As it moved forward, it smashed into the lights hanging from above, shattering each with the impact. The scene before him looked as if the darkness was stalking in on them, destroying all light in its path.

He took aim with the M4 and unleashed a barrage of 5.56 ammo into the beast, but it didn't even slow from the bullet strikes. He knew that every round had struck its target, but the thing kept coming.

The door continued to grind shut, but it wouldn't be closed before the creature was on top of them.

Knight's mind fought for a solution.

The M4 had a mounted grenade launcher that would surely slow the beast's progression, but the resulting explosion would also be likely to seal the passageway and trap them inside the shelter like a tomb.

But then, he caught sight of a fire extinguisher mounted along one side of the tunnel. He took aim at the extinguisher and waited for the right moment as the beast approached.

He forced his thundering heart to calm and released his breath as he sighted in on his target. He would only get one chance at this, and if he missed, they would all be dead.

Just before the massive shadow overtook the extinguisher, he squeezed back on the trigger. The M4 barked fire and propelled a line of hot metal toward the red extinguisher.

As the bullets struck, the compressed contents of the device broke free. White foam exploded outward, covering the beast.

The massive shape shrieked and swiped at its face. It stumbled forward and to the side, and slammed its head against the wall.

Within a couple of seconds, it was back on its feet and charging forward.

But the distraction had bought them enough time.

The hatch swung shut and sealed with the sucking sound of pressurization just as the beast closed in. He could hear the creature roaring from the other side. The hatch shook, and dust rained from the ceiling as the monster tried to tear its way inside.

After a moment, the scraping and banging noises ceased, and both sides of the hatch were completely silent.

Knight released a long breath and turned back to the frightened faces of the children. "Everyone okay?"

The two children just stared wide-eyed at the hatch without acknowledging him. He couldn't see any blood and all of their limbs were intact. He wasn't a shrink; if they made it through this alive, the therapists could deal with shock. He had to contend with more important matters.

He glanced around the space behind the children, but it was obscured by darkness. He scanned the side wall of the bunker and reached out to flick a switch. Overhead fluorescent lighting hummed to life with a hiss and snap.

He stepped forward and surveyed the inside of the bunker.

"This isn't a bomb shelter," he said.

8.

At least forty flat panel monitors populated the wall in front of Knight. A long gray Formica desktop in front of the monitors contained five workstations, each with a black leather rolling desk chair, a transparent keyboard dotted with Chinese lettering and a trackpad. Knight reached out and pressed a random key at one of the stations. The forty monitors instantly blinked to life. Images of the city rotating from different angles and orientations filled the screens. From the camera views, he guessed that some were mounted on buildings and some were roadway cameras stationed on traffic signals.

"What is all this?" Ling said. "It's like looking through God's eyes."

Knight found the comparison somewhat frightening, considering the amount of power the operators of this system held. "It's some of type of urban video monitoring system. I've heard of several systems like this being implemented back in the United States. They're used to monitor traffic patterns, track criminals for the police, monitor for crimes in progress. That kind of thing."

"Is that where you're from? America?"

"Yeah, I'm an American."

"Really? You don't seem like the way my Uncle described Americans." He felt her eyes climb up and down his now-dirty cream-colored suit. "What's it like there?"

He could just imagine the horror stories of the evil and immoral American capitalist regime that had been drilled into Ling's head. "It's a great place where people are free to live their lives the way they choose."

The girl's eyes sparkled at the thought. He knew that such a vision of a perfect America where freedom rang and everyone was treated equally wasn't entirely accurate, but it was a sufficient one-sentence answer. Plus, he didn't have time to give a politics lesson, and the ultra-idealized version of America was much closer than the lies he suspected she had been told her whole life.

As he scanned the monitors, his thoughts shifted to the scheduled rendezvous with the rest of the team from Delta. He had no idea where he was supposed to meet them. That information had been lost along with Mueller. For a moment, he considered how he could get in contact with them. He needed to warn them about the beast.

"Ling, have you seen any other people in the city? Other soldiers maybe?"

The girl's eyes darted away, and she seemed to shrink.

"What's wrong?"

She swallowed hard. "We were living in a building north of here when we heard men screaming and lots of shooting. We went to see what was happening." She hesitated. "That's when we first saw the monster."

He closed his eyes and thought of all the soldiers he had seen die in combat, all of the families back home that would receive notices of their loved ones' deaths but never know the classified details. They would never know that their family members died as heroes defending the world from forces beyond imagining.

He opened his eyes and looked to the bank of monitors. "Ling, can you show me the building where you heard the screams?"

9.

Ling examined the walkie-talkie that Knight had found on a shelf in the back of the bunker, twisting it over in her hand and studying each knob and button.

"Are you sure that you understand everything?" Knight said.

Ling nodded and repeated his instructions. "If Jiao or I see anything on the monitors, then we call you on the radio. And don't touch any of the knobs because you've already dialed in the proper frequency."

"That's right. And whatever you do, don't leave this bunker. You'll be safe here. There's food and drinks in the back." He had already searched through the rest of the chamber and found that it apparently did pull double duty as a bomb shelter. There was a storeroom in the back that held enough supplies to sustain at least a dozen people for a week. He suspected that it was designed to hold the top city government officials and their families in case of an emergency. The kids would be safe here for a long time while he dealt with whatever enemy waited outside.

He moved to the first workstation and brought up the camera feed of the hallway outside the bunker. The beast was gone, but he had spent the past hour trying to locate it on any other camera and had come up with nothing. He suspected that it was out there somewhere waiting for him, but he couldn't stay holed up inside the bunker forever. He had a job to do.

If the team from Delta had gone up against the creature, then the chances they were still alive was slim, but he had to know either way. And maybe he could at least gather some intel from the scene to shed light on what exactly he was up against.

"Once it's safe, I'll be back to get you both out of here."

"Please," Jiao said. "Don't leave. Don't go." The boy struggled to keep his emotions in check. Tears welled in his eyes. His voice shook. But he stuck his chin out, doing his best to appear tough.

Knight knew the kid had been abandoned, first by his parents in death, and then by the betrayal of an abusive uncle, but there was no way he could stay with the kids. Nor could he take them along for the ride and keep them safe.

Knight crouched in front of the boy. "I have to go," he said. "Not because I want to, but because I have to. It's the only way any of us will get out of this mess. Understand?"

A furtive nod confirmed the boy's understanding.

"You have Ling," Knight said. "She's never left you, right?"

Another nod.

"And she's kept you safe? You trust her?"

"Yes."

"Then trust her now. And me. I won't leave you here. I promise."

Ling and Jiao both reached out and hugged him tightly. His cheeks flushed at the unexpected display of affection. He patted them awkwardly on their backs and then said, "Okay, stand back and shut this door behind me."

He raised the M4 and then pressed the red button next to the bunker's entrance. Gears whirred and the seal of the door popped as the hatch slid open. He moved into the hallway and turned back to the kids. Fear and doubt were etched onto their faces. He gave them a thumbs up and a nod. Ling reached out and pressed the button. He stood there and watched until the door was completely closed. Then he set off toward the rendezvous point.

The staging area had been set up within some type of warehouse surrounded on all sides by a high chain-link fence. During the journey, he had tried to move invisibly from cover to cover, but there was no way to avoid being completely exposed as he made his way to the warehouse. The ability to easily see an attack coming was likely one of the reasons that the Delta team commander had chosen the spot.

He scanned the surrounding buildings for a few moments, but he didn't see any signs of enemy activity. Slinging the M4 over one shoulder, he took three deep breaths and braced himself. Then he took off in a dead sprint toward the tall fence.

He hit the fence with a jump and began to gracefully scale the barrier. Within a second, he was at the top. One arm shot over the peak, and his fingers grasped the other side. In one fluid motion, he flipped over and dropped to the ground. He hit the pavement of the warehouse's parking lot in a roll and came up with his sidearm at the ready. The weapon's aim followed his eyes as he scanned his surroundings for danger. Seeing no threats, he moved toward the warehouse.

The structure was a large, white block building with a green metal roof fronted by loading docks and tall garage doors designed for semi-trucks. A red and white realtor sign adorned the front window along with a sign detailing the features of the property. He hit the building's wall next to the window and cautiously scanned the interior. The door was unlocked, and he pushed inside. The office space was vacant of everything except a large reception desk built into the wall.

He holstered his Beretta and unslung the M4 rifle. Then he moved down a hallway past a string of empty offices and men and women restrooms. At the end of the hall, he pushed through a door into the main section of the warehouse.

The smell of rotting meat assaulted him immediately. The buzzing of flies filled the space with a constant hum like the pulsing of a large generator. The warehouse had become a charnel house. Bodies of the soldiers were strewn everywhere. Some had been torn apart. Others had apparently been tossed across the room like rag dolls, their limbs twisted at strange angles, their mouths bent open in silent screams. Empty shell casings coated the floor, stuck in the congealing blood.

The sights, sounds and smells attacked his senses and overwhelmed him. He lost his breath and stumbled back into the hallway. His emotions and gut instinct told him to flee from this place as quickly as possible and never return, except maybe in his nightmares. But his training as an elite soldier told him to move forward and complete the mission. And without searching this room, he wouldn't even know what the mission was.

He pushed back into the warehouse, trying to focus upon the task at hand and look at the scene objectively. He needed intel and equipment. The thought of any of these people still being alive was a near impossibility, but he decided to check each anyway. He moved through the room, checking each body first for a pulse and then for papers or gear.

One of the bodies, the remains of a woman, had long brown hair and a beautifully sculpted frame. He wondered if this was some type of civilian scientific or intelligence advisor. The lifeless form was lying face down against the pavement with the hair spread out concealing the woman's features. If he had been forced to bet, this body would have been his pick as possessing useful intel.

He crouched over the woman, reached out, and grabbed

hold of her right shoulder. Then he rolled her over onto her back.

As she turned over, her arm came up, and Knight found himself staring down the business end of a 9mm Sig Sauer pistol.

10.

With a speed born partially out of instinct and partially out of an intense training regiment, Knight slapped the gun away from his face just as it spit fire. A round shot past his head and clanged off the metal ceiling.

In one motion, he rolled away and pulled his own sidearm. His finger flew to the trigger, but he resisted the impulse to pull.

He recognized the face staring back at him.

The woman's name was Anna Beck. She had been a member of the Gen-Y security force hired by Manifold Genetics, the company that had tried to harness the power of the Hydra. She had also been instrumental in the company's downfall and had even earned herself the temporary callsign: Pawn, during the incident.

Beck raised her hands in surrender and allowed the Sig Sauer to slip from her grasp. It thudded to the concrete but remained within her reach.

He held his aim for a moment and then lowered his own weapon. "Every time we meet, you aim a gun at my face."

She smiled. "Sorry about that. I heard someone coming and thought you might be whoever was responsible for...this."

She gestured to the carnage that surrounded them.

He regained his feet and held out a hand for her. She took it, and he pulled her from the ground. She stood at least five inches taller than he did, and she was still every bit as beautiful as he remembered. He hadn't seen her since she'd fled the scene of Chess Team's confrontation with Manifold Genetics at the *Alpha* facility in New Hampshire. She'd helped defeat her employer, but had probably feared prosecution. The team would have vouched for her, and Deep Blue would have likely pardoned her, but not even the team knew their handler was the U.S. President at the time. But Knight had thought of the tall woman with "girl next door" good looks on occasion, wondering what happened to her. He'd hoped to see her again, but envisioned the reunion a bit differently than this.

He looked her over. She wore black BDUs that reminded him of those he had seen the SAS, Britain's Special Air Service, use. She pulled her brown hair back into a ponytail and secured it with a black band.

"So you don't know what happened here?" he said.

"No, I only got here a few minutes ago."

He wanted to trust her, but he kept his weapon ready at his side as a precautionary measure. "Why are you here, Beck? What the hell is going on?"

She stretched out her arms and rotated her neck. It issued an audible pop. "I was forcefully recruited by a team of British commandos for my knowledge of Manifold. We were supposed to meet up with an American team from Delta, but the Americans abruptly broke contact. So a group of three SAS commandos and I went on a little recon mission."

"Where are the others from your group?"

She shook her head. "I don't know. I was on point. Then, I turned back and they were gone. Vanished. No sound, no screams, no gunfire. Three men…just gone."

He thought of how quickly Mueller had disappeared. But

the pilot was at least able to get off a few shots. "Okay, that's explains why you're here, but not what the hell is going on. Why are any of us here in the first place?"

A strange expression filled her face. "You don't know?" Then she looked him up and down, taking note of the expensive suit. "And what are you wearing?"

He sighed. "I'll explain later. Right now, I need answers. Unfortunately, I only know what I've gathered for myself. I was basically shanghaied into this mess and was told that I'd receive a full briefing once I arrived here." He held out his arms at his side. "As you can see, that's not going to happen."

She chuckled and shook her head, but there was no happiness or humor in the gesture. "I guess I'll be the first to welcome you to hell, Knight. Why don't we get away from this smell and head back into one of the offices. Then, I'll explain what I know."

He nodded his assent, and they headed back toward the door to the office area. He tried to keep his eyes from the mutilated bodies of the fallen soldiers as he went. He ignored the implications of the scene and what it meant for their chances of survival on this mission.

His hand reached out for the handle of the office door, but he jumped back as a frantic voice crackled to life on his radio. In a voice punctuated by fear, Ling said, "Knight, we saw it— the monster. It's coming toward you."

11.

Knight scrambled among the bodies, searching for anything that they could use against the behemoth headed their way. A tarp hid a large stack of wooden boxes in the center of the staging area. He pulled the tarp free and scanned the boxes for any labels. He smiled at a symbol etched into the side of one of them. The box carried no other markings or labels, but the small symbol gave him all the information he needed. The symbol was that of a chess piece. *A knight.*

He pulled a four inch folding knife from his pocket and snapped it open with a flick of his wrist. He used it to pop the top off the crate. Inside was a set of weapons and ammunition: a Barrett XM500 .50 caliber sniper rifle, a fully auto version of the FN FS2000 for close quarters combat and an AA12 fully automatic shotgun loaded with FRAG-12 high-explosive armor-piercing shells. He assumed that he had Deep Blue to thank for the specially selected equipment.

A line of three black Humvees sat untouched along the back wall of the warehouse. He directed Beck to grab an end of the crate, and they quickly loaded the ordnance into the first of the Humvees.

"You're driving," he said. Then he moved toward the first

of garage doors and found the button to open it. He pressed it, and the massive door began to slide up.

When the bottom of the door reached eye level, a flash of movement from outside registered in his peripheral vision.

He rolled to the side just as a massive claw swung down and sparked against the concrete. It was at moments such as this that he was thankful for his small stature and graceful speed. A bigger man might have been torn in half.

The M4 barked to life as he unloaded upon the hulking figure, but the beast barely registered the attack and seemed to regard the bullet strikes as a minor annoyance. As it slowly looked him over, Knight had the distinct feeling that the creature was playing with him. But this allowed him, for the first time, to receive a clear view of his enemy. He didn't like what he saw.

It stood at least nine feet tall and seemed almost as wide. Every limb of its enormous body bulged with sinewy muscle. It wore the shredded remains of black BDUs and moved like a man. But its arms hung low, and its skin was covered with greenish iridescent scales. Its ears were almost human but were deformed and pointed like those of an iguana. Sharp claws tipped the massive five fingered hands, and a bulbous, elongated and hairless head sat upon muscular shoulders and held a snouted face, yellow eyes and a mouth full of gleaming, curved fangs. It reminded Knight of some freakish coupling of a man and Hydra.

He had seen enough. He unleashed a barrage of fire into the creature's eyes. It stumbled back and Knight tried to move away, but within a few seconds, the damage to its face had repaired itself.

A low rumbling that seemed all-to-similar to laughter emanated from somewhere deep within the creature's throat. The sound filled Knight with dread. The more he saw of this beast, the less it seemed like an animal. And the more it seemed almost human.

The thing made no more advances toward him, but as he inched toward the Humvee, it shadowed him. He knew that if he took off he'd never reach the transport before the beast tore him to shreds.

It croaked out another short laugh and then drew back a giant clawed arm.

He prepared to leap away and kept his eyes locked with the creature's, hoping that its eyes would choreograph its movements.

The sound of screeching tires drew its reptilian gaze back into the warehouse just before the black Humvee slammed into the creature's side. Beck accelerated with the beast clinging to the front grill of the vehicle and hissing in a way that no longer seemed human at all.

Knight watched as the Humvee barreled across the parking lot, burst through the fence and slammed into the concrete wall of a neighboring building. He ran after the damaged vehicle, and after a few seconds, the Humvee pulled back from the wall.

Beck screamed, "Grab on!"

He didn't have to be told twice.

He leapt onto the running board and grabbed hold of the vehicle's frame. "Go!"

Beck slammed her foot to the floor, and the Humvee sped away. Knight swung his legs up through the window and slid inside the vehicle. Then he moved to the hatch in the transport's roof that was normally used by the gunner. The well-oiled hinges swung open easily, and he poked the upper half of his body into open air.

He looked back to where the beast should have been splattered against the wall, but instead of a bloody smear, he saw the thing stumble back into the street. The monstrous face turned in his direction. The impact had caved in half of its head, and one of its arms had been severed cleanly above the elbow.

But before his eyes, the face began to reform, and a new limb sprouted from the bloody stump.

The thing bent back its body and roared. The two wing-like ears on either side of its head slapped against its skull when it roared, creating a distinct rattling sound Knight remembered all too well. The shriek was full of rage and agony and made Knight feel very small and helpless. After a few seconds, the beast lunged onto all fours and charged after them.

Knight ducked his head back into the cab of the Humvee and said, "I think we're gonna need a bigger boat."

Beck glanced in the rearview mirror. "I think we're going to need a few Apaches with Hellfire missiles."

12.

The old man had lost track of time as the days, nights and weeks of imprisonment had begun to blur together. He wasn't sure how long he had been in this place, and he no longer cared. Giuseppe Salvatori reached up to his face and rubbed through the thick gray beard. He felt an odd sense of shame at his shabby appearance. He had always prided himself on his hygiene. Before this, in all those years since he was a teenage boy, had he went a single day without shaving? He didn't think so. The thought of dying in such a dreadful state filled him with sadness.

Most people found themselves imprisoned due to their shortcomings or mistakes, and Salvatori thought it amusing that he was imprisoned because of his genius and his skills in genetic science. Years earlier, he had mentored a brilliant young man named Todd Maddox. That same young man had gone on to crack the secret behind the legendary Hydra. But before doing so, he had also acquired a position for Salvatori within Manifold Genetics. He had no way of knowing at the time that aligning with his former pupil would eventually bring about his own downfall.

The meager space he had come to call home wasn't exactly

a dungeon from days of old. It was merely a concrete supply closet within a research bunker that had been equipped with an electronic locking mechanism to protect sensitive equipment and data. Of course, this meant that it also contained no cot or toilet, and he had been forced to endure the indignity of sleeping on a mattress on the floor and defecating into a five-gallon bucket that sat in the corner. The bucket didn't get emptied often, and he imagined that the stench would overwhelm anyone who entered. He had grown accustomed to the smell long ago.

Salvatori heard footsteps in the hall just before a blinding light flooded into his cell. He strained for his eyes to adjust to the sudden illumination. The man that stood before him was impeccably dressed in a gray pinstriped suit that probably cost enough to feed a third world country for a week. Round wire-rimmed spectacles rested upon a small upturned nose, and the man's salt and pepper hair was parted neatly and slicked back from his face. Salvatori wondered why Phillip Cho would dress like that when he worked alone. Behind the glasses, Cho's eyes were bloodshot, and Salvatori could see the residue of a white powder beneath the man's nose. Cho carried himself like some sort of aristocrat, but Salvatori knew that Cho was no less of a monster than the abomination that he had created.

"I have nothing to say to you," Salvatori said, his voice dry and brittle.

Cho's face showed disgust, either from the show of insolence or from the smell. He shook his head and made a clucking sound with his tongue. "I really hate to see you like this. Don't you think it's time that we end this little game?" Cho moved farther into the room, leaned against the wall, and crossed his arms over his chest. "I know that you can fix the serum. You hold the key. Maddox was your pupil, and if he could unlock the secret to immortality, so can you. It's time that you share your secrets with me, old friend."

Salvatori raised his eyes to meet Cho's. "If I were thirty years younger..."

Cho laughed. "Too bad that you're not thirty years younger. Maybe you were smarter back then. Now you're just a stubborn old man that refuses to listen to reason. I don't want to have to hurt you, but I will. I'll make you beg me for death. Do you understand? I'm out of time, and so are you."

Cho reached into his jacket pocket, and the locking mechanism of the door clicked open. He stepped into the frame of the doorway and then turned back to Salvatori. "You had better think about what I said. The next time I set foot in this place, I will have my answers."

As Cho turned away, Salvatori quickly gained his feet and lunged out toward the younger man. He grabbed a fistful of Cho's suit and struck him in the stomach, but the punch was weak and ineffective. Cho swept out a foot and tore Salvatori's feet out from beneath him.

The old man hit the concrete, and Cho kicked him hard in the midsection. Salvatori's vision filled with white spots as his breath was stolen from him. He clutched his arms into his chest and curled into a ball.

Cho swept a hand back over his hair and said, "Damnit, old man. We've been given the opportunity to remake the world, to do something that's never been done. We could be gods."

Salvatori coughed hard and sucked in a lungful of air. "You're insane," he said in a wheeze.

Cho chuckled and kicked the old man again. "It's always been said that there's a thin line between genius and madness. I'm going to check on our son's progress, but I'll be back soon. We'll finish this discussion, and if you don't help me, you'll see firsthand how insane I can be."

With the threat still hanging in the air, Cho walked out the door and slammed it behind him.

Salvatori waited a few moments before he moved. Then, still crumpled in a ball on the floor, he raised his hand to his face and examined the small device that he had stolen from Cho's jacket.

He cursed under his breath. The device must have struck the ground when he fell and damaged the transmitter. He closed his eyes and sighed. But then he willed himself onward, popped the back panel from the device and set to work.

13.

Knight grabbed the AA12 automatic shotgun from the crate and slapped on a 32-round drum loaded with explosive shells. He popped back up through the hatch and judged the distance to the creature. Beck was pushing the vehicle at a quick and steady speed. The lack of vehicles and pedestrians on the road made it possible for her to do so without swerving in and out of traffic and throwing off his aim. Somehow, the beast was keeping pace.

"How much farther to the SAS camp?" he called down into the cab.

"Probably another couple of miles."

"Radio ahead and tell them that we're coming in hot."

The radio at his belt squealed to life. "Knight, are you okay? We're scared."

He grabbed the radio from his belt and said in a flurry, "Everything's fine. I just have to deal with a little pest problem."

He sighted in on the beast loping along behind them, pushed out a breath and squeezed the trigger. The weapon kicked hard against his shoulder and three explosive rounds shot forward and struck the beast dead center in its chest and head. Small explosions bloomed to life and halted the creature's momentum, driving it backward and off its feet.

But Knight knew that it wasn't out of the fight.

"Stop the truck!" he said.

To Beck's credit as a soldier, she didn't question his orders, and the large, black vehicle skidded to a halt. The smell of burning rubber mixed with the aromas of gunpowder and burnt flesh filling the air.

The beast was already pulling itself from the ground, the jagged wounds in its abdomen sewing themselves shut. He sighted in again and unleashed a steady barrage of fire. The butt of the rifle hammered against his shoulder, and it took considerable strength to keep his aim from drifting skyward.

He kept the trigger pulled back until the shotgun clicked empty and the entire cylinder of explosive rounds had wreaked havoc upon the creature's body. The small explosions blew the beast back in a bloody mess, howling in agony. Its ruined flesh lay in pieces scattered across the pavement.

The keening wail was like a hot needle in his ears. The pain had to have been beyond imagining—more than any man or beast should ever have been forced to endure. But right before his eyes, the bloody pieces of flesh began to reform outward from the creature's core.

He shook his head and called down to Beck. "Get us out of here."

14.

The SAS had positioned their staging area within the loading dock of a large building designed for use as a shopping mall. But all of the storefronts were bare and their signs blank. Light red bricks dotted with white bricks that came together in artistic shapes when viewed at a distance, composed the structure. It appeared to be a sizable multi-tiered complex with half of the space stretching up three stories high, plus a basement. The loading dock sat on the back half of the building in a carved out niche that opened into the basement level. Two stories of empty shops and food stands rested above the bank of waist-high doors designed for trucks to pull against and be quickly unloaded. An enormous parking lot sat behind the loading docks. There wasn't a single car on the lot. In fact, Knight had seen no more than five vehicles since he had arrived in the city.

Beck parked in the lot close to the entrance, and they walked up a ramp and into the loading dock. Knight felt the itch on his skin of eyes staring down gun sights. Beck carried one end of his crate, and he held the other. He had given her the AA12 and strapped the FS2000 over his shoulder. He kept the weapon at his back and tried to make his movements delibe- rate and non-threatening. He had enough problems without worrying about a friendly-fire incident.

As they pushed through the door, the black-clad SAS soldiers swept from the shadows and fell in around them. They weren't being overtly aggressive. Their weapons remained pointed at the floor, and they tried to make their movements seem casual. But he could plainly see that the SAS boys were ready to take the two of them down at the slightest hint of trouble. He could see their fingers coiled tightly around their weapons, and the sweat beading up on their foreheads.

An angry voice called out in a thick Scottish brogue. "Where the bloody hell're my men, Beck? And who's your friend?"

The man stepped out from behind a long table containing an assortment of maps and gear. He wore black BDUs and carried himself like an officer who had seen his fair share of combat—tight and efficient yet relaxed and confident. A black beret covered reddish brown hair, and the flesh on the right side of his neck was mangled from a nasty burn scar.

"Your men are gone," Knight said. "And we're next unless you listen up."

Surprise fell over the man's face, but his eyes quickly narrowed into angry slits. There was a bulge of chewing tobacco in his front lip, and he spit a black liquid stream onto the floor. Knight saw the man bite back an angry comment, as the officer looked him up and down. Instead, he said, "Okay, I'm listening."

"I'm American spec ops. The rest of the U.S. team is gone. Killed by the same thing that took out your men. It's big. It's nasty. And it's tougher than anything you've ever come up against."

The SAS commander snorted. "Quite frankly, kid, I don't know you, and you don't know me. So don't talk to me like I'm one of the sodding paper pushers. I've probably spilled more blood in more mud than your whole damn unit combined."

Knight rolled his eyes. The old-timers always looked at his smooth, handsome face and assumed that he was some kind of newbie. And they didn't have time to swap war stories and compare scars.

Beck said, "You should listen to him, Donahue. He's experienced in situations like this. You've heard the reports of what attacked those bases."

Donahue waved her off. "I've heard the horror stories, but I've yet to see any hard intel to back them up. Just you showing up here with some stranger making a bunch of wild claims."

Confusion contorted Knight's features. "What are the two of you talking about? What bases? What attacks?"

Donahue gave him a strange look. "I thought you were with the Americans?"

Beck said, "He got dropped into this mess without being briefed. Donahue, just have your men keep an eye on the perimeter, and we'll all play a little game of show and tell."

Donahue nodded to one of his men standing in the shadows nearby, and the rest of the SAS team scattered. Beck stepped forward and laid the AA12 on the table. "Okay, Knight. Let's start from the beginning. Since the Hydra incident, I've been tracking down other illegal activities being conducted by Manifold Genetics. I'd been hearing rumors that one of the scientists escaped from the *Alpha* facility with a sample of Hydra blood. My sources said that this man, who was of Chinese decent, had decided to go to work for his homeland developing the possible military uses for the Hydra DNA. He had recruited another former Manifold employee named Giusseppe Salvatori, who is one of the world's foremost experts in genetic recombination. Salvatori has done quite a bit of work with reptilian DNA. He's also an old friend of mine. He must have heard that I was trying to track down what Manifold was up to because he tried to contact me."

"What did he say?"

"All his message said was that he needed to speak with me and that the world was in great danger. Needless to say, that got my attention—especially from someone like Giusseppe. He's a very practical man. Unfortunately, I never heard from him again. Neither man popped back onto the grid after that, at least so far as I could tell."

"Until now."

Beck nodded. "Two days ago a British clandestine military outpost and a secret American research facility were wiped out. The only transmission received described a creature that couldn't be killed. That's when the SAS brought me in as a consultant."

"Like I said, a crazy horror story," Donahue added.

"I wish that were true," Knight said to Donahue then turned back to Beck. "How did you trace things back here?"

"That was your American friends," Donahue said. "They used some surveillance satellite logs to backtrack the path of a transport chopper that landed near their base. When our governments each learned that the other had also been attacked, this became a joint operation."

"So the chemical spill explanation for the city's evacuation was bullshit."

"Which our governments suspected anyway. They just didn't know the whole story."

Knight put his fists flat on the table and leaned over. "And we're here to fill in the blanks and get to the bottom of this mess."

Donahue straightened up and said, "I still don't buy the story about some bloody monster that can't be killed. I know science today can seem like magic, but how the hell is something like that even possible."

Knight thought back on the explanations for the Hydra's abilities that he had been given. He shrugged and raised his hands, unsure of how much classified information to share with the man. "I'm not a scientist, but I know that all life on the planet shares something like ninety-eight percent of the same genetic structure and our DNA bonds in pairs. All of those genetic pairings are glued together with water. But this thing's DNA is glued together with something called heavy water or D20. It's this abnormality that allows its DNA structure to contain genes not found in other organisms. Some of those extra genes give it unique regenerative capabilities, among other things."

Donahue looked at him like he had just recited an epic poem all in Latin.

"Salamanders," Knight said. "Squid. Lizards. Starfish. They can all re-grow severed limbs or tails. This thing can do the same thing, but on a much grander scale and very quickly. You don't really need to know how it does this, only that it can. And you need to adjust your tactics to compensate."

The SAS commander opened his mouth to speak but didn't have time to utter a single word before a flustered member of his team ran up to them. Fear showed on the SAS soldier's face, but he still tried to maintain a modicum of respect and composure. The man was breathing hard, and the spaces between his words were punctuated by sharp intakes of air.

"Major Donahue, we've lost contact with the outer perimeter guards, and we've spotted something big headed our way."

15.

"What do you mean something big?" Donahue said.

The man diverted his eyes. "It looks like… I've never seen anything like it."

Knight leaned into Donahue's field of vision, blocking his view of the other soldier, and said, "You need to bust out the biggest guns you have and prepare for the fight of your lives."

Donahue hesitated a moment. His face still showed a level of suspicion and doubt. But then he moved toward the front of the loading dock and started barking orders to his men.

Knight pulled the top from his crate of weaponry and ammo. He took out another 32-round cylinder of explosive shells for the AA12. He mounted the drum onto the rifle and yanked back the weapon's slide. Then, he held out the large, fully automatic shotgun to Beck. She took it without a word. "That's all the ammo I have left for that gun. Make them count."

"What about you?"

He smiled. "I've got another toy that I'd like to take for a ride."

She nodded and ran off to join the others in defending the perimeter.

He reached back into the crate and retrieved that Barrett XM500 sniper rifle. The weapon fired a round capable of blowing a man in half from over a mile away. Once the weapon was ready, he grabbed for the walkie-talkie at his belt. "Ling, do you see the monster now?"

After a moment of static, the voice on the radio responded. "We see it! It's coming your way."

He didn't bother to respond; he was already on the move. He sprinted to one of the loading doors and pressed the button to open it. The roll-up door began to rise, and after it had cleared about a three-foot opening, he pressed the button again. The door's upward climb ceased.

He dropped to his knees and then went prone with the sniper rifle still in his arms. His hope was that a well-placed .50 caliber round through the creature's brain stem would be enough to finally take it down. But there was only one way to know for sure.

The creature loped forward on all fours, running like a mountain gorilla. The fact that the beast didn't seem to fear them at all and was charging into a nest of highly trained and heavily armed commandos didn't fill Knight with very much confidence at their chances of survival. But he'd always agreed with Wayne Gretzky when the hockey legend said that you miss one hundred percent of the shots you don't take.

Instantly and instinctively adjusting for wind, distance and speed, Knight took a breath, pushed it out, and squeezed the trigger. The rifle bucked, and the massive bullet sliced a path to its intended target. In a spray of red mist, the impact struck the creature, halting its headlong charge. Through the scope, he could see the bullet wound blossom in its neck. The trunk-like legs fell out from beneath the beast, and its momentum carried it forward, skidding across the pavement of the parking lot.

The SAS team cheered as they witnessed the shot through their own scopes. He ignored them and refused to breathe while scanning the creature for movement. It lay still for what seemed like a long time, and he allowed a small hope to creep into his mind.

The feeling evaporated, however, as the beast began to twitch. Within a few seconds, it pulled itself to its feet and shook its head from side to side like a dog that had just run into a sliding glass door.

The group fell silent as the beast continued its charge. He stood up and pressed the button to close the garage door back down. Donahue appeared at his side.

"What the hell is that thing?" Donahue said in a whisper.

Knight chuckled. "Welcome to my world."

16.

Knight dropped the XM500 sniper rifle onto the table, shook his head in disgust and turned to Donahue. "Major, you need to have your men hold that thing back for as long as they can with whatever they've got."

Donahue didn't question him and started calling out orders to his men. Once in position, he yelled for the men to fire at will, and the loading bay filled with the sound of gunfire and spent shell casings striking concrete. The SAS soldiers were calm and professional, firing in short bursts to conserve ammo and slow the creature's progression.

Knight grabbed Donahue by the elbow and pulled him back to a spot behind a stack of crates that partially shielded them from the cacophony of fire. "We can't put a stop to this little science experiment with that thing on our asses at every turn."

Donahue shook his head and spat more brownish liquid onto the floor. "There must be a way to kill that thing."

"Unless you brought along a tactical nuke, I think we're SOL."

Donahue cocked his head to the side. "What's SOL?"

"Shit out of luck."

"Right. If we can't kill it, how about trapping and containing the beast?"

Knight squeezed his eyelids together and rubbed at his temple. "That's a good thought, but the creature is incredibly powerful. Even if we could trap it somehow, where would we hold it? Do you have air transport out of here? Maybe we could re-equip and come back with a plan?"

"Sorry, mate. We parachuted in, but the Americans were going to bring an Osprey for aerial support."

He thought back on the way his day had begun and the Osprey spinning out of control and plummeting toward the ground. "The Osprey is out of commission. Trust me, I was on it when it went down."

Donahue cursed under his breath, but then his face lit up. "We might not have a nuke, but if we can make it to that Osprey, we might have the next best thing."

"What's that?"

Before Donahue could answer, Beck ran up and said, "We've lost sight of the creature!"

Donahue spun toward the perimeter. "What do you mean you lost sight of it? Where the hell could it have gone?"

Knight saw the next few seconds pass in slow motion.

Beck's eyes were wide with shock. She shrugged her shoulders, showing that she was just as confused as Donahue. Then the skylight above their heads crashed inward, glass exploding down all around them. A dark shape fell through the hole in the ceiling amidst the rain of shattered glass.

17.

The beast dropped the forty feet to the ground. Knight not only heard the crunching of shattered glass as the monster struck, but he also heard the cracking of the creature's bones. It howled and fell over on its broken legs. But within a matter of seconds, it was back on its feet.

The SAS commandos wheeled around and opened fire. The beast didn't seem fazed by the barrage of hot metal. It rushed forward and tore into the line of soldiers.

The distinctive sound of the AA12 filled the air as Beck pushed the creature back. It toppled over and careened into a stack of crates. But Knight knew that it would only buy them a few seconds. He grabbed Beck by the arm and called out to Donahue. "Pull your men back!"

He pointed Beck toward the loading bay door. "Open that up. I'll grab one of those." He gestured toward a pair of tan HMT 400s resting along the back wall. The strange-looking vehicles were the primary troop transport used by the SAS. They reminded Knight of small fire trucks with no front glass and guns mounted on top instead of hoses.

Beck nodded and ran off toward the bay doors while Knight sprinted over to the transports. He knew their only hope was to outrun the creature, and despite the HMT 400's bulky appearance, the vehicles were fairly agile and capable of speeds in excess of fifty miles per hour.

He ran amid the deafening sounds of gunfire. The bright flashes in the darkened space sliced into his eyes, white spots filling his vision.

He tried to ignore the screams of the SAS soldiers as the creature tore them apart. He attempted to keep his mind focused upon the task at hand, but the sights and smells of the warehouse that had contained the bodies of the American team kept appearing within his mind's eye. An odd sense of guilt washed over him that he had failed to spare the SAS group of the same fate.

Hurdling obstacles, he cut through the confusion of the attack to reach the vehicle. It was just in front of him, and he reached to grab on and pull himself into the HMT's driver seat.

But a giant shape fell in front of him, knocking him back.

The creature stared down at him with fire in its eyes. Again, the beast seemed strangely human. It seemed to have realized that he had caused it a great deal of pain and was ready to return the favor.

It backhanded him across the room like a rag doll.

He slammed into a stack of nearby crates. The pain exploded in his mind, but he fought to regain his feet. He looked up to see the beast charging at him and knew that it would be on top of him before he could stand. Instead, he kicked his legs and tried to back away on his hands and backside. He rolled his legs up just as the creature pounded the concrete in front of him. The impact shattered the concrete and sent him rolling away.

He hadn't even gained his bearings by the time the creature was on him again. He felt the beast's fist clamp onto him like a vise, its talons slowly digging into the meat of his shoulder.

It lifted him from the ground and pulled him close to its fang-filled mouth. It roared with satisfaction. He could smell the rank stench of death on its breath as it stretched its jaws wide and moved in for the kill.

But then, he recognized the all-too-familiar blast of a .50 caliber rifle and felt himself falling as he watched the beast's head jerk to the side in a spay of blood. He rolled as he hit the ground and stumbled forward, trying to put as much distance as possible between himself and the creature's bloodlust.

His legs felt heavy, and the world spun. He fell to his knees and looked up to see Beck fire another blast from the XM500 rifle. Then, Donahue and one of his men were at his side, lifting him from the floor. He shook them off and grabbed his FS2000 from the table.

Donahue said, "Retreat! Fall back into the mall!"

They scrambled through the docks toward the customer section of the mall. Donahue kicked through a doublewide loading door, and Knight and Beck followed on the man's heels. The remaining SAS soldiers were close behind. Knight could hear the sound of suppressing fire coupled with screams as the spec ops team fell one by one.

Calming grays and whites complemented the side of the mall that would one day be seen by the world. Three open stories stretched above their heads, and there were spots reserved for fountains and fancy displays. But the fountain was empty, and the displays were non-existent. A warren of stairs and escalators stretched to the sky. The stores were hollow white shells of glass and drywall. Knight was amazed at the wastefulness of the whole city. What kind of a government would build empty cities to falsely bolster an economy built upon the backs of the poor?

Donahue urged the group forward. Knight heard roaring behind them and turned see the front of a store burst inward as the creature threw one of the SAS soldiers through the plate glass. He grabbed the XM500 from Beck and blasted a round into the creature's skull. It crashed backward, destroying the front of another empty store.

They ran forward as fast their legs would carry them, curving around bends and forks in the path and heading toward the front of the mall. But the place was huge, and it seemed like they'd already run for miles. He had conditioned his body into a finely tuned machine, but even Knight could feel the fire in his legs and the burning of lungs that begged for air. They couldn't keep this up much longer.

Then the front entrance loomed ahead, and they were pushing their way into the open air. He didn't dare glance over his shoulder. He could almost feel the creature's hot breath on his neck, and he prayed that it was only his imagination.

Ahead, Beck called them toward a manhole cover in the street. "Help me!" she screamed.

Knight, Donahue and the last of the SAS soldiers grabbed hold of the cover and willed their remaining strength into pulling the heavy metal free from the ground. The others started to climb down, and Knight turned back to the front of the mall.

The mall's face was two stories of shimmering glass surrounded by shrubbery and brick. Before Knight's eyes, the glass burst outward. The upper panels cracked and fell from their supports. The pieces of shrapnel erupted everywhere, and he shielded his eyes.

The beast stood where the glass had been. It threw its arms out to the side and bellowed at its fleeing prey.

Then, it charged.

Donahue and his man were already on their way down the ladder, but Knight knew that he and Beck would never make it if they took the time to climb down. *Time for the express elevator*, he thought. Knight wrapped his arms around Beck and jumped into the hole as the beast skidded over the opening.

The pair landed upon the two SAS commandos, and they all fell together in a heap on the sewer floor. Knight gained his feet and pulled them back, just as a clawed fist swiped down through the opening above. The creature slashed back and forth and stretched out after them. It jammed its head and arm down, but it couldn't fit its enormous, muscular torso through the opening. It shrieked at them in rage. Then, the creature pulled its bulk back from the opening and disappeared.

The four of them stood there a moment, leaning against the sewer walls and trying to catch their breath. Donahue leaned over with his head in his hands. "If I would've listened to you sooner..." His voice trailed off.

Knight shook his head. "It wouldn't have made any difference. There's nothing we could have done."

Donahue looked to the sky. "Maybe. Maybe not."

"Come on," Knight said. "Let's get out of here before it finds a way down."

They set off through the sewers in the direction of the downed Osprey with Knight taking point and Donahue watching the rear. As they passed under the next manhole cover, a beam of light burst down on them.

A giant talon followed through the hole as the creature shrieked and slashed at them.

Knight flopped to the ground as the clawed fist fought toward him. It grabbed onto the ladder and tried to yank itself through the opening. Its red eyes looked down at Knight, and their gazes locked.

It stopped its shrieking, and its mouth peeled open to reveal rows of razor sharp fangs. Saliva dripped down from the hungry maw. It slowly raised its arm back through the opening, but it continued to stare down at him. He could feel something being passed between them. It wanted him to know that this was far from over, that it *would* kill him.

He stared back at the beast and matched its animosity.

This thing had taken the lives of good soldiers, and he wanted its head as much as it wanted his blood. He gave the beast a two-fingered salute. It snarled back and then disappeared.

18.

Salvatori surveyed his handiwork. It was a shabby patch job, but it didn't really matter as long as it worked. The small device resembled a garage door opener with large flat button and a slot on its back where a clip could be inserted to allow it to attach to a belt.

He pointed the device at the door to his cell and held his breath. If it had been damaged beyond repair and didn't function, he knew that he would have no choice but to give Cho what he wanted. He had no illusions that he was tough enough to withstand the kinds of torture that a mind like Cho's could dream up. He would crack, and the world would die along with his resolve.

He knew that Cho wouldn't recognize that the remote for his cell's locking mechanism was missing until the next time he returned. The door automatically locked when it was closed, and Cho had already opened it from the inside when Salvatori stole the device from the younger man's jacket pocket. The maneuver had been expertly choreographed; he had spent plenty of time alone in a cell considering how to best accomplish the deed. He also suspected that Cho's mind was too burned out from all of the drugs to allow for rational thought.

He closed his eyes as he pressed the button. His heart seemed to stop as there was no sound for a second, but then a small click of the mechanism signified his deliverance. He breathed a long sigh of relief. Emotions overwhelmed him, and he nearly wept. But he didn't have the luxury of savoring his new found freedom. Now was not the time for celebration; it was the time to set things right.

19.

There was no sound within the sewers or on the streets above, and they only had one small flashlight between them. A pale halo of illumination lit the path ahead. The air was moist but stagnant. The sound of their movements bounced off the tile walls and created the illusion of footsteps at their backs. Their voices echoed down the tunnel, and they spoke in hushed tones for fear that the beast would track them by the noise.

Knight found the sewers oddly clean. But he supposed that he should have expected that, since hardly anyone other than maintenance workers had ever lived in the city. "So Donahue," he whispered. "You mentioned that we might have the next best thing to a nuke. If you've got some kind of plan, now would be a good time to share."

"I don't know if I'd call it a plan, but if we can get to that Osprey, we should find a little something to even the odds."

"I checked the weapons hold, and there wasn't anything there other than small arms."

"This little toy is mounted under one of the wings, not in the hold. We didn't know what kind of enemy base we would encounter out here, so we asked the Americans to bring along the ultimate bunker buster. A thermobaric warhead."

Knight was familiar with thermobaric weapons. They were powerful explosive devices that used a two-stage detonation process. The first stage blew the casing of the bomb and released an explosive chemical vapor into the air that expanded out and filled all the surrounding space. Then, the second stage ignited the accelerant and flash-fried everything within the blast radius. The explosion literally set the air on fire. The final effect was a massive concussion wave that would crush anything that hadn't been turned to ash. Thermobaric warheads were the most powerful non-nuclear weapons in the U.S. arsenal.

It would surely be enough to kill the creature. There wouldn't be a single cell left to regenerate. But there was a problem.

"It would do the job," he said, "but the EMP attack that took down the chopper would have fried the warhead's electronics. Without the detonator, it's just a big paperweight."

"I've been thinking about that. If you can get me there, I'm pretty sure that I can make it work."

"Pretty sure?"

"You have any better ideas?"

"I was giving some serious thought to bugging out and heading to the beach with Beck, but I suppose we could give the warhead thing a shot."

"I don't know," Donahue said. "I wouldn't mind seeing her in a bikini."

Beck stopped dead in her tracks and glared back at the pair of them. "If you two Don Juans think that creature is a force to be reckoned with, then you've obviously never seen me pissed off."

Donahue raised his hands in mock submission and moved back with his man. Knight moved up and walked with Beck. "From what I can tell, no one has seen much of you over the past few years."

"You've looked?"

"I might have Googled you once or twice."

Beck grinned. "I've kept a low profile. I think you know why."

"Actually," Knight said. "You have no reason to hide."

Beck turned a curious eye toward him.

"The events at Manifold *Alpha* are classified. Chess Team has taken over the facility. Ridley topped the most wanted list for a while, but—"

"Ridley *survived?*"

That's right, Knight thought. The last time Beck saw Ridley, he'd flung himself from a helicopter several hundred feet in the air.

"He'd taken the serum. He survived the fall and a whole lot more. We caught up with him, though."

"Where?"

"You wouldn't believe me if I told you."

She perched her eyebrows high on her forehead. She wanted to know.

"Plus, then I'd have to kill you."

Her disappointment was easy to see, but he couldn't tell her about Babel, he mother tongue or how the world was nearly enslaved by Ridley.

"What's important for you to know is that your name isn't on any agency list. There are no warrants for your arrest. You're not even on a no-fly list. You're clean."

"So you really aren't looking for me?"

"Me, as in the U.S. government? No. Me, as in *me*? Let's just say I'm not disappointed to have found you. Though the circumstances could be improved."

Remembering they were hiding from a killing machine similar to the Hydra sobered Knight. He moved on in silence, hoping to continue the conversation later, if they survived.

20.

Phillip Cho peered down through the lens of the Zeiss and Olympus microscopes at the sample of Hydra DNA. Then, he re-examined his notes. If only the sample he had collected hadn't degraded as he made his escape from the Manifold *Alpha* facility or if he could have procured Todd Maddox's actual findings. *Or*, he thought in disgust, if he had been given access to the equivalent of five NSA Cray Triton supercomputers capable of handling three hundred twenty billion instructions per second as Maddox had.

He cursed and shoved the papers from the lab station. The area around him contained some of the most sophisticated genetic research equipment in the world: automated karyotyping and fluorescence in-situ hybridization stations, low-temperature freezers, barocyclers, automated Vysis VP2000 slide processors, Axon Scanners and Thermotrons. Despite all of the fancy equipment though, he couldn't find a way to retain the benefits of the serum without inducing the terrible side effects, namely turning into a human-reptile hybrid like his pet, Huangdi.

Creating Huangdi hadn't been easy, but with Salvatori's help, they were able modify a porcine circovirus—a single-stranded DNA virus—for use as a carrier. The virus crossed the cell membrane of the host cells and infected them with the DNA alterations from the Hydra-derived serum. The infected cells divided, the virus spread and the host was transformed on the cellular level. Huangdi had been the product of several generations of trial and error, but Cho still couldn't determine the specific genes necessary for regeneration only. Todd Maddox had cracked the code, but Cho hadn't been one of the inner circle, so he wasn't privy to the genius's methods. The truth was that he had never been much of a scientist, but he refused to allow those shortcomings to rob him of his true destiny.

His creature, who had once been a Chinese soldier, was named for the first legendary emperor of China. At the end of his reign, the original Huangdi was said to have been immortalized into a dragon that resembled his emblem, and then ascended into heaven. Cho's pet dragon had an undeniable usefulness from a military standpoint, but the serum could be used for so much more.

It could quite possibly grant immortality.

It could change a man into a god, if only he could harness its power and filter out the negative effects. But his handlers within a small, but powerful cell of the Chinese government were short-sighted and ignorant. They didn't care about furthering that line of research at the moment. They were preoccupied with the concept of an indestructible army of monsters that could crush their enemies. What they refused to consider is that countries and borders come and go, but with his serum, he could be eternal. He could be like the first emperor. He could become a dragon, figuratively speaking, and ascend to heaven.

He had been briefed on their ultimate plan. First, they would smuggle his super soldiers into the United States and position them at strategic locations across the country. Then they would strike from within and cripple the superpower.

While the majority of the Chinese government, controlled by cultural elitists who viewed anything non-Chinese as barbaric, was satisfied with simply maintaining control of China, the splinter group he worked for saw things differently. They didn't just want to expand Chinese control of other nations; they wanted to destroy those nations, claiming their land, resources and wealth for the exclusive use of the ever growing Chinese population. That Chinese laborers working for American corporations couldn't even afford proper housing was infuriating enough. But when their own government loaned the United States $1 trillion dollars, the group saw this as a grave betrayal—one that required a bold response. Once the war began, the rest of the government would fall in line and the Chinese people—all of them—would benefit from the reclamation of the wealth they were now giving away.

Once their biggest barrier was eliminated and America was reduced to rubble, they would sweep over the rest of Asia, the Middle East, Africa and Europe. At which time, their ultimate goal of a one-world communist government would be complete.

And, of course, Cho would have his pick as to where he wished to be regional governor. He would be a king. But somehow, that just wasn't enough for him. Why be a king when you can be a god?

But he would also need an army to enforce his will, and before they would provide him with the resources necessary to birth his children, they wanted an insurance policy. They were afraid of what could happen if they built an indestructible army, even they had no method of combating. It was sound thinking, and Cho couldn't mount any argument against it. He wondered if they suspected his true motivations.

Either way, he had no intention of developing their anti-serum that would halt the rejuvenating capabilities of his soldiers. Instead, he had focused all of his time and energy on creating a new serum that would transform his weak, mortal body.

He knew that Salvatori held the key, but the old man was too stubborn. Although, Cho had already considered a few methods that he could employ to open the old man's mind and make him more cooperative.

He looked to the clock and wondered how long it had been since he had slept. He supposed that it didn't really matter. The moment for resting was long past. Time was against him now, and he couldn't allow it defeat him. He couldn't allow himself to fail when he was so close.

Almost with a mind of its own, his hand shot out to his desk drawer and retrieved his supplies. He laid the mirror on the workstation and dumped out the white powder. Then he sliced it into neat lines and snorted it up one nostril. He dabbed the excess onto his finger and rubbed it into his gums. His head dropped back against his chair, and his eyes fell shut. He sat there for a moment and let his medicine do its job.

When his eyes opened, he felt much better. He felt ready to take on the world. With the press of a few keys, the images on his bank of monitors changed to views of the empty streets of the city. He pressed another string of keys to bring up Huangdi's location using his GPS tag. The screen showed that no signal was being received from Huangdi's tracker.

Unfortunately, he had been unable to find a way to create indestructible communication hardware for use with his indestructible monster. Although Huangdi's flesh would heal, any radio or tracking devices could easily be destroyed.

He dialed up the recordings for the areas surrounding the SAS camp. A click of the mouse and the images spun backward in high speed. Another click and the screen showed Huangdi's attack on the British encampment. Cho marveled at the creature's abilities and its brutality. It was truly an efficient killing machine. Maybe he could find a way to leave intact some of the Hydra DNA code that related to strength and agility in the final serum.

He watched on the recording as a small group escaped from Huangdi's grasp and made their way into the sewer system. It was hardly of any concern. Huangdi would hunt them down and finish his mission. Cho had no doubts about that. It was what the creature had been conditioned to do: complete the mission at all costs.

But the escape wouldn't look good on his video reports, so he pulled up the files in a video editing program and cut off the last section before sending it on to his superiors. Then he moved to another workstation within the lab that had been equipped with the most recent in video conferencing hardware and software.

A light blinked on next to the camera, and within another few seconds, General Kuan Yin appeared on the screen. Cho bowed respectfully to the General and said in Mandarin, "General, the field tests are proceeding very well. I'm sending over a set of video files that demonstrate the potential of the weapon I've created. As requested, for this final weapons test before we move into production, I have drawn in some of the most elite fighting men that our enemies have to offer. We attacked two clandestine bases operated by the U.S. and Great Britain and then allowed them to track us back here. They reacted as we had anticipated and sent in teams from Delta and the SAS. As you'll see from the videos, the skills of these men made little difference. No human being can stand against my soldiers."

The General gave a curt nod. "Very good, Dr. Cho. But how is the anti-serum progressing?"

"It's very near to completion, sir."

The general's eyes narrowed into slits. "You've been telling us that for a while now. I hope there have been no setbacks in your work. We need that anti-serum immediately, or we will be forced to terminate the program."

Cho fought back his disgust and forced a smile. "Everything is moving along well. You'll have the anti-serum in hand very soon."

"Very good. You are a true patriot, doctor. And you will be rewarded as such, once your work is complete."

Cho bowed graciously and then cut the connection. As soon as the light blinked out, he spit onto the blank monitor. *Rewarded. True patriot.* He suspected once he outlived his usefulness and delivered the serum and anti-serum, the general or one of his lackeys would erase him from existence. After all, they couldn't have him giving away any of their secrets to a rival government.

Yes, they would try to kill him. Unfortunately for them, he was one step ahead.

21.

Knight's radio chirped to life, and the sudden sound in the dark, quiet space caused him to instinctively step back and reach for his weapon. The voice on the other end said, "Knight, we're getting really scared. We can't see you on any of the TVs. Are you okay? Are you coming to get us?"

He grabbed for the radio and said, "Everything's fine, Ling. I told you that I'm a monster hunter. And I think we've found a way to kill this particular monster. Once it's over, we'll all be able to go home."

There was a moment of silence, and then Ling said, "We have no home."

Knight winced. Of all the insensitive, asshole things he could have said, he picked one of the worst. He thought of Fiona—the adopted daughter of Chess Team's field leader, King—and the love that every member of the team shared for the girl. But despite his affection for Fiona, he had always been glad that the true burden of being her father had fallen to King. It wasn't a job that he had ever wanted or even considered. His comment cemented the fact.

He wished he could offer them a solution, but he wasn't child services. He was a Black Ops soldier fighting monsters—

human and non-human around the world. Fiona had been forced into their world by the threat on her life, but Chess Team wasn't an orphanage. Still, he felt for the kids. He knew what growing up without parents was like. But they were tough. And they had each other. They'd pull through.

When he opened his mouth to speak, his voice sounded dry and cracked. "Umm…we can talk about that once we're all safe."

He looked up to see Beck watching him from the corner of her eyes. She was grinning. "You've got a beautiful smile," he said. "Wouldn't mind seeing it on a more regular basis."

The eyes narrowed, but the grin remained. "I bet you would."

"After all this is over, maybe we could take a little trip together. I know a private spot in the Cambodian jungle where two waterfalls meet. At sunset, the rays of light shine through the falls and create the most beautiful rainbow you've ever seen. I'd love to show it to you."

Beck stuck her finger down her throat and made a gagging sound.

"Okay…I could take you to Montana instead. We could kill a grizzly bear."

She cocked her head to the side. Her brown hair fell over the side of her face. "You're getting closer, but I don't know. I've never dated a guy that's shorter than I am."

"I could wear heels if it helps."

She chuckled. The gesture projected a softness into her eyes. "It might."

Donahue cleared his throat loudly. Knight noticed for the first time that the SAS commander was limping slightly and favoring his left side. Donahue coughed and said, "We're here. If you love birds are done twitterpating, maybe we can kill that bloody creature now."

22.

Knight scanned the area above the manhole cover using a fiberscope. Nicknamed a snake cam, the device was a long, flexible bundle of fiber-optics with an eyepiece at one end and a lens at the other. It was an invaluable tool used by spec ops soldiers to recon a room or area without alerting the enemy to their presence. He saw no sign of the beast on the street above and grabbed for his radio. He was getting used to having Ling and Jiao watching his back. They were beginning to remind him of miniature versions of Deep Blue.

"Ling, are we clear to move up?"

"I think so. But we don't see the monster on any of the other monitors, either."

He knew that just because they couldn't see the creature, didn't mean it wasn't up there somewhere waiting for them. But he had little choice but to proceed despite the risk. The last of Donahue's men, a corporal named Jenkins, joined Knight on the ladder, and they pushed the cover free of the opening. The group moved cautiously over the street and up through the parking garage. Apparently, their escape through the sewer had been successful in throwing the beast off their trail. Once on the roof of the parking garage, Donahue set to work at dismantling the warhead. Knight, Beck and Jenkins kept their eyes on the perimeter. But there was no sign of the creature. The air was calm and still. The city, despite its warren of roads and skyscrapers, was eerily silent.

After a few minutes, Donahue called Knight over and gestured toward the open contents of the thermobaric weapon. "The warhead's remote detonation control circuitry is fried, and the power source is shot to hell. I might be able to rig something up and bypass the damaged circuitry, but the power source is out of my hands. We're going to have to find a replacement."

"Like what? What can we use?"

Donahue shrugged. "Almost anything above a flashlight battery could work. It doesn't need that much power to spark the detonation."

He thought for a moment. "What about a car battery?"

Donahue nodded. "That'd do the trick. Too bad there aren't any left in this bloody parking garage."

"That would be too easy, but I do remember seeing an abandoned car down the road a bit near where I first encountered the creature." He put a hand on Donahue's shoulder. "Get this thing ready to blow, and I'll take care of the rest."

"You got a deal, but you had better get those little legs of yours pumping. It's only a matter of time before that thing tracks us here."

"Little legs?"

Donahue shrugged and turned back to the warhead.

Knight climbed into the Osprey. The interior was the same jumbled mess that he had seen earlier, but this time, he knew where to look. He had seen the items he needed when he had broken into the weapons locker. He retrieved a small box from the cockpit and a can of emergency fuel attached to the back of the dead ATV. He dumped out the regular gasoline from the can and went to the side of one of the Osprey's reserve fuel tanks. Then, using a hydraulic hose taken from the wreckage, he siphoned out some of the craft's JP-8 jet fuel.

As he dropped down from the side of the ruined aircraft, Beck's eyes passed over the items in his hands. "What's all that for?"

He smiled. "A little surprise for our big-ass friend."

23.

The beast watched from high above the streets of the ghost city, scanning for its prey. It burned with hatred for the small things that kept stopping it from completing the objective. Why did the small things keep hurting it? All it wanted was to complete the task that the master had assigned. The objective was all that mattered, all that it had left.

There was a time when there was more. Strange, fuzzy pictures like something from a dream occupied its memory. It saw images of a man, a soldier, a proud patriot. It saw the soldier as a boy fishing with his grandfather on Taihu Lake, and his mother taking him to the Temple of Heaven—a sacred place in southern Beijing where emperors in the Ming and Qing dynasties worshiped and offered sacrifices. Then it watched the boy grow to manhood and train to serve his country. It saw the soldier with a woman and a baby.

But after that, the only memories it could recall were pain, rage and the objective.

It remembered all these things, but it couldn't make the connection as to why. Where did these images come from? What were they? It felt deep sadness and anger, but it didn't truly understand either emotion.

All it knew was that it had to obey the master. It had to kill.

A scent carried on the wind drew its attention, and it leapt from rooftop to rooftop, tracking down the source of the smell. Then it saw the small thing running along the road below. This one was the worst of all the small things. This one had caused it much pain. But no more.

It was time to complete the objective.

24.

Salvatori tapped furiously on the keyboard. The glow of the single flat screen monitor illuminated his pale and weathered features. All around him, Cho's equipment hummed with life. A part of him pitied Cho. The man didn't realize that, despite all of the technology in the world, a person couldn't solve a complex puzzle without a keen mind and a clear focus. He knew that Cho was little more than a wannabe scientist with a drug addiction and possessed none of the qualities necessary for true success.

He finished the final stroke, and his finger hovered over the Enter key. He closed his eyes and let his finger fall. The countdown on the screen began to tick away the seconds. When the time reached zero, the facility's fail-safe system would be activated—a small thermonuclear device designed to annihilate their creation if the creature were to become compromised in some way.

He found it strange that he wasn't more frightened by his approaching death. He no longer cared about his own life. While he had sat alone in his cell, he had had ample opportunity to look back on his life and the choices that he had made along the way. He now knew that his involvement with Manifold Genetics, and in turn, this project were mistakes so large that they exceeded his ability to ever rectify them. He had been blinded by his own ego, among other things: breaking new ground in science, ushering the world into a new era, leaving behind a legacy, fortune and glory. The road to hell truly was paved with good intentions. His vision for the future had been corrupted, and now the greatest thing he could hope to accomplish with the last moments of his life was to undo all that he had done.

He closed his eyes and felt great satisfaction that within a short time everything would be set right. He had been unable to bypass the fail-safe's countdown and detonate it instantly, but he had succeeded in disabling all of the system's announcements and notifications. He had also disabled the de-activation mechanism. Unless Cho specifically checked, the man would never know that his death was approaching until it was upon him. And even if he did discover that the fail-safe had been activated, Cho wouldn't have time to crack in and stop the detonation.

Salvatori pushed away from the desk and exited what was once his lab. He moved down a long, white hallway toward the bunker's exit. He had one item left to accomplish, and then his victory would be complete. Cho had a personal transport, a specially modified Sikorsky S-92 helicopter, located on the roof of the adjoining building. He needed to disable the helicopter to ensure that Cho couldn't escape with his research if he learned of the bomb's activation.

Salvatori was only a few feet from the exit when Cho stepped around the corner from one of the adjoining hallways. Cho held a Norinco QSZ-92 semi-automatic service pistol in his left hand. The weapon was leveled at Salvatori's chest. A wide grin cut across the maniacal young man's face. The whites of his eyes were blood red. His breathing was fast and erratic.

"I'm proud of you, old man," Cho said. "I didn't think you had it in you."

"You'd be surprised how much fight is left in this old dog,"

Salvarori said, thinking of the countdown ticking down even as they spoke.

Cho issued a high-pitched chuckle. When he spoke, his words came out slurred. "It doesn't matter now, anyway. You see, I went to retrieve you from your cell, because I want you to bear witness to my ascension."

"What are you talking about? You've lost your mind."

"Come, come, come. I'll show you." Cho gestured toward his lab with the gun. "I've done it, old friend. I've cracked the code to immortality. You're going to watch me become a god, and then you're going to die."

25.

With the can of JP-8 jet fuel in his left hand, the FS2000 in his right and a couple of tools in his pockets, Knight ran in the direction of the abandoned car. He could feel the beast's eyes on him. The sound of movement registered high above on his left, but he didn't turn.

Then a thunderclap sounded on the pavement behind him, and his legs trembled from the sudden shockwave. The beast roared at his back. But still, he willed himself not to turn around. Not yet.

He pressed forward as fast as his legs would carry him, his own footfalls being drowned out by the heavy tread of the beast.

His heart throbbed against the walls of his ribcage, and his lungs burned with fire.

The pounding of the beast grew closer and closer—nearly on top of him.

He could see the creature from his peripheral vision in the reflections on the glass fronts of the surrounding buildings. When the distance was just right, he spun around and tossed the can of jet fuel into the air above the creature.

Simultaneously, he squeezed back on the trigger of the FS2000 and unleashed a barrage of 5.56mm rounds into the sailing can. He knew that despite what was shown in the movies, bullets didn't spark and ignite fuel. Instead, the can filled with holes, and its contents rained down on the beast.

It paid no attention to the attack and continued its loping charge.

Knight stood his ground, staring directly into the reptilian, yet oddly human eyes.

Then, at the last possible second, he dove to the side and rolled away.

The creature's momentum carried it forward past the spot he had just occupied. He shot to his feet and pulled out the flare gun he had retrieved from the Osprey's cockpit.

The beast shrieked and wheeled around.

Knight sighted in and fired.

The fiery projectile rocketed forward and struck the beast squarely in its chest. In a brilliant explosion of flame, the jet fuel covering the creature's body ignited.

The beast howled out a cry of agony the likes of which Knight had never heard before. Although its wounds were healing, it still couldn't extinguish the accelerant-fueled flames, and the fire was consuming its flesh as fast it could regenerate. It thrashed wildly around the street, slamming into the buildings and smashing through the glass facades. Then it sprinted away, its prey apparently forgotten.

Knight had no idea how long the fire would keep the creature distracted, so he didn't waste a moment of time. He discarded the flare gun and rushed toward the abandoned vehicle.

The car, a new model Hyundai Elantra, had been tire-locked, most likely by one of the city's few law enforcement officers who had nothing better to do before being evacuated. He checked the driver's side door. The first rule of breaking and entering was to always check to make sure that the door wasn't already open. In this case, it was locked, so he used the butt of the FS2000 to break in the window. The hood release sat to the left of the steering column just under the kick panel. He pulled the release and moved to the front of the vehicle.

He fumbled a bit to open the hood and found much of the engine hidden beneath by a black engine cover. But he'd come prepared. Using a ratchet, he quickly removed the cover and tossed it to the side along with the bolts. With the battery exposed, he went to work with a wrench, loosening the retaining bolts and pulling the cables free from the positive and negative terminals. With everything loosened, he reached in and took hold of the battery.

His heart was throbbing so loudly in his ears that he mistook the sound for the heavy footfalls of the creature. A part of his mind kept picturing the beast closing in on him, its talons extending toward him, its razor sharp teeth ready to tear into his flesh.

Then it was over, and he had the battery cradled under his left arm. The whole process took nearly two minutes, but the threat of being torn apart made it feel like hours. It was Hyundai's own brand of battery that probably came with the car, and he prayed that it still held enough juice to detonate the warhead.

He sprinted toward the site of the downed Osprey. He didn't know how long the beast would be occupied by his fiery distraction, but he hoped it would buy him enough time to reach the others and set the trap. Because either way, he knew that the next time he saw the creature, one of them wouldn't make it out alive.

26.

Phillip Cho punched a key on his keyboard, and a three dimensional molecular model of the newest generation of his serum appeared on the seventy-inch display mounted on the wall. He pointed toward the screen and said, "Behold, the key to immortality."

Out of curiosity, Salvatori moved forward and studied Cho's work. After a moment, he laughed.

Cho's face was a mask of confusion and disgust. "What's so funny?"

"This serum won't work. In fact, it's likely to kill anyone foolish enough to attempt its use. I see what you were trying to do, Phillip. You hoped to stop the onset of adverse effects by reducing the replication rate of the circovirus and the manner in which it inserts the foreign genetic material. But all this will accomplish is a more drawn out and painful transformation. Plus, you've inadvertently removed the restriction placed upon the virus's incubation period. We engineered the virus so it would die off once the transformation was complete. But with this, the virus will not stop. It will continue to spread, and the subject will continue to change and grow, likely to the point that the circovirus destroys the poor creature from the inside out. Or worse. I wouldn't even dare to predict the effects that something like this would have upon a living host."

Cho stood there for a moment. The confusion etched onto his features. His eyes darted between the display and Salvatori. Then the look on his face turned from confusion to anger, and he slapped Salvatori hard across the jaw. The old man cried out and toppled backward to the lab floor.

"You're lying!" Cho screamed. "You're just trying to trick me. And I won't let you stand between me and my rightful destiny. Nothing will stand in my way!"

Salvatori could see that Cho was beyond rational thought, and nothing he could say would convince the man that what he was attempting was insane. Salvatori used the corner of one of the workstations to pull himself up and said, "Fine, Phillip. Test out your serum. I'd prefer it if you killed yourself anyway."

Cho's mouth curled into a snarl, and he shook with rage. "How about I kill you first?"

Salvatori watched the pistol buck in Cho's hand and a line of flame shoot from the gun's barrel. It took him a moment to register that Cho had just fired the weapon. It took another moment to feel the pain in his abdomen.

He suddenly felt light-headed. He touched a hand to his side. It came back smeared with red. He reached out to grab the table, but he missed and crumpled to the floor.

Cho smiled down at him. "Don't feel bad, old friend. We can't all live forever."

From his place on the floor, Salvatori watched as Cho retrieved a syringe from the table. "Here's to immortality." Cho plunged the needle into his arm and pushed the amber-colored liquid into his body.

Cho stood absolutely still for a moment. Then he said, "I can feel it. I can feel myself changing! It's working!" The look on the younger man's face was euphoric at first. He laughed uncontrollably and spun round in a little circle.

But then his limbs started to shake. His arms clutched around his abdomen, and he doubled over. "No. What's happening?"

Using the distraction to his advantage, Salvatori dragged himself across the tile floor toward the exit. At his back, Cho began to scream. There were no words that he could understand. It was a feral howl of agony spoken in the language of pain. He refused to look back. He focused on the door ahead, and within a moment, he was in the hallway.

The screaming continued within the lab along with the sounds of shattering glass and breaking equipment. The change would be slow and terrible. He pitied the man, but he had tried to warn him. Although many would say that Cho had gotten what he deserved, Salvatori knew that no man or beast should ever to have to die like that.

27.

The pain had become its world, agony extinguishing all thought and drenching its mind in chaos. It fought against the madness and searched for a way to make the pain stop. It shrieked out for help. It slammed against walls and rolled on the ground, but nothing seemed to break the hold that the agony had upon it.

Its vision came and went, giving it only scattered, incoherent glimpses of its surroundings. It could feel the eyes melting within its skull and then reforming. It would be granted a second's worth of sight, and then the darkness came again. Then the process repeated itself over and over.

But then, through the flames, it saw something ahead. A dock. A lake. Water.

It charged blindly forward until it felt the ground disappear beneath its feet. Then the cool water washed over it, extinguishing the flames. Relief flooded its mind along with other strange emotions that it could not fully comprehend. It allowed itself to sink slowly below the waves and into the depths of the lake.

After a moment, its lungs cried out for air, but it didn't want to leave the soothing cocoon that had rescued it from the pain. It fought against the urge to breathe for a few moments longer but then acquiesced, and its gigantic limbs clawed for the shore. It grabbed hold of one of the dock's wooden support pillars. Talons dug into the wood, and hand over hand, it hauled itself onto the dock's surface.

It laid there for a moment on its back. Wispy clouds shifted through a light blue sky. They masked the sun, but it could see the light from the giant star illuminating the edges of one section of the canopy.

A flash of memory shot before its eyes, and it realized why the small thing it had been had volunteered to become something more. It remembered the fire now. It remembered burning. It remembered the immense pain. But it wasn't a memory from this life. It was from a time when its flesh didn't grow back, a life where it had a wife and a little boy. It caught a glimpse of their faces with surprising clarity. It fought to remember their names, but the effort made the memory of their faces fade away.

It knew that they had died somehow but couldn't recall the details. The emotions surrounding their deaths were still intact, however, especially the guilt. It realized that it was to blame for their deaths. Its flesh had been badly scarred, and it had spent a long time in some sort of hospital.

Gradually, the memories dissolved back into some inaccessible part of its mind. It fought for them. It closed its eyes and tried to remember the little boy and the woman. But they were gone. And all that remained was the objective, piercing its consciousness like a thorn.

It knew then that it couldn't change the past or what it had become. All it could do was complete the mission. Or perhaps the small things would finally succeed in killing it. A part of it, the part that remembered, hoped for death and a release to the pain that had become its life.

28.

Knight scanned the streets surrounding the parking structure. The beast couldn't be far behind. He had returned with the battery a few moments ago, and Donahue had quickly set to work in preparing the bomb. He just hoped that they would be able to draw in the creature and contain it long enough to detonate the warhead.

He reached for the radio, clicked on the receiver and said, "Ling?"

A frightened voice replied in a flurry of words. "We're here. Can we leave now? Are you coming to get us?"

"We're almost ready, Ling. We've got a plan to kill the monster. Just stay where you. This nightmare is about over."

"Okay, Knight. Please hurry."

"I'm on it, kid. See you soon."

The children were understandably frightened, but they had also showed a great deal of strength and fortitude from the first moment that he met them. He felt a strange sense of pride even though he could take no responsibility for instilling such strength in them. He suspected this might be what it felt like to be a parent. He had never wanted kids; they weren't compatible with his lifestyle. But for perhaps the first real time in his life, he wondered if he was missing out on something by not settling down and having children of his own.

"Knight, come over here," Donahue said at his back. He gave the perimeter one last check and then joined the SAS officer next to the downed Osprey.

"I got the hot dogs and marshmallows all set. You ready to light the fire?" Knight said.

Donahue nodded. "Aye, we're ready to deep fry that big iguana, but we've got two problems. One, I have no bloody clue of how we're going to keep big ugly in range of the bomb long enough. It needs to be contained right here at ground zero. We can't take a chance of the blast wave blowing it clear and having it regenerate on us."

Knight thought for a moment and then said, "Leave that to me. I'll keep him pinned here. What's problem number two?"

Donahue smiled, but it wasn't an expression born of joy or humor. It was the type of smile that a person would display at a funeral to the grieving widow. "The detonation mechanism is trashed, but I was able to hot-wire the warhead to be detonated manually. Somebody'll have to stay behind and trigger it."

Knight stiffened and looked deep into Donahue's eyes. "No, there's got to be another way. Too many have died already. Either we're all going home or none of us are. We could—"

Donahue held up a hand to stop him and then opened his flak jacket. A jagged wound carved through his abdomen. Blood soaked his clothes and the interior of the jacket. It looked as if a black substance had mixed with the blood. "I caught a stray round in the side. Went right in under my body armor. I'm not gonna make it, Knight. This bloody thing killed my men, and I'm going to take it down. When I see my boys in the next world, I want to tell them that I showed that thing that you don't screw with the SAS."

Knight smiled and gave Donahue a slow and solemn sa-lute.

A roar sounded in the distance. The beast was coming.

"You better get going, Knight. You just pin that thing down, and I'll blow it all to hell."

29.

As they ran toward the distant skyscraper, Knight heard gunfire and clanging noises coming from the top of the parking structure. Corporal Jenkins turned back and said, "He's in trouble. We've got to go back and help him."

Beck grabbed the remaining SAS officer by the arm before he could return to Donahue. "He's fine. He's just trying to draw in the creature. And if we're not ready when it finds him, then he's going to die for nothing. You want that?"

The corporal stared back at the building without a word. Knight could sympathize with the man. He had no idea how he would react if it were King up there preparing to take his final breaths. "Come on, Corporal. Let's make him proud."

Jenkins stood there a moment longer and then turned back to the skyscraper. He took off in a sprint with Knight and Beck on his heels.

As they ran, Beck said, "Are you sure that building is out of the blast radius?"

"Not really, but I hope so."

"That's great. Your confidence makes me feel all warm and fuzzy."

"I tell you what," Knight said, "let's make a little wager."

"I can tell that I'm going to regret asking, but what do you have in mind?"

"Nothing too complicated. If I get you out of this mess alive, then you go wreck diving with me. And you wear a bikini while we do it."

She gave him a strange look and raised both eyebrows.

He thought back on what he had just said and added, "I mean…while we dive."

"Fine. But if I'm the one who gets you through this alive, then you get to wear the bikini."

Knight was about to complain, but realized that either way, she was agreeing to join him. Distant gunfire ruined the moment and pulled him back to the present, spurring him forward.

30.

Donahue succumbed to a fit of coughing after a few moments of screaming and banging on the hull of the Osprey. It felt like his chest was on fire and his lungs were caving in. He felt light-headed, and the world pulsed and throbbed along with the beating of his heart and the pounding in his skull. When he looked down at the hand he had coughed into, he found it slick with blood.

He leaned his head back against the Osprey's fuselage and allowed his eyes to slip closed. He felt so tired. He just needed to close his eyes for a moment to recharge his battery. Just close his eyes for a few seconds and he'd be fine.

He jerked his head up and slapped himself across the face. If he fell asleep now, he suspected that he'd never wake up. A soldier's will to fight was all that he had left. His men deserved to be avenged, and he refused to let them down.

A few more rounds from his pistol sailed into the distance. His screams lasted until his lungs had no more power, and then he used the butt of his weapon to clang against the bottom of the Osprey.

Where the hell was that thing?

He feared that he'd already be dead by the time it came to

kill him. That would be no fun for anyone.

He pulled himself to his knees and checked his work on the warhead one last time. Everything looked in order, and he allowed himself to slip back down to the pavement.

Then he saw a clawed hand reach over the top of the concrete lip of the parking structure. It pulled itself up slowly and then sat there watching him.

Its eyes darted around the wreckage as if checking for some kind of trap. It was the first time that he had seen the creature show any kind of caution. Apparently, Knight had made an impression with his distraction.

The creature's eyes settled back on him. Fury burned in the red, reptilian spheres, and the beast hissed softly.

"Do you worst, you ugly bastard," Donahue said.

The creature's massive legs stomped slowly forward, and its lips peeled back in a snarl. As he studied the gleaming white fangs, Donahue prayed that Knight was in position and ready to keep up his end of the plan.

31.

Knight took aim at the beast through the scope of the XM500. He estimated that his vantage point was right at one and a half miles from his target, meaning that he was beyond the effective range of the weapon but still within its maximum boundaries. It wasn't easy to hit a target from one and a half miles. A huge number of variables had to be considered—wind, distance, drift, the curvature of the Earth—and there were only a handful of people on the planet that could make such a shot.

Thankfully, he was one of them.

He made the necessary adjustments in his head, released his breath and squeezed the trigger.

Through the eye of the scope, he saw the beast flop to the side from a direct hit to the cranium. He shifted his aim to Donahue and felt a pang of remorse for the man, but also felt proud to have known him. Only the rarest men could look death in the face and not cower in fear. The device utilized a two-stage explosion, so they needed to make sure that the beast couldn't escape before the second stage was activated. The first stage would blow the casing and disperse the accelerant, fluoridated aluminum layered between the charge casing and a PBXN-112 explosive mixture. The second stage would detonate the fuel, and anything not incinerated would be crushed by the resulting shockwave.

Knight watched Donahue prepare to detonate the first stage just as the beast gained its feet. It must have sensed some type of danger. It seemed almost fearful. He sighted in and fired again, keeping the beast pinned down and unable to escape.

It flopped to the side but continued to crawl toward the edge of the building.

Most any living thing would be destroyed within a mile of the blast, but with this creature, he wanted to be sure that it was as close to the eye of the storm as possible to ensure that every last cell was annihilated.

The beast pulled itself up and tensed its legs to jump clear.

Knight fired again, but then a blinding light filled the eyepiece of the rifle. He jerked his head away, white spots filling his vision. The thunderous boom arrived a moment later, shaking the air from his lungs. A wave of warm air coursed over his body, pushing dust and debris away from the blast-zone. After a moment, he looked back to see the mushroom cloud rising into the air above the spot where the parking structure had once stood.

At his side, Beck said, "If that didn't kill that thing, then we might as well just give up and head to the beach."

"Sounds about right to me. Let's just make sure everyone else gets out alive, first."

She nodded.

He looked back toward the center of the fireball. It wasn't just the creature that had died. A good man had gone with it. Jenkins sat with his back against the wall, facing away from the blast. Knight leaned over and placed a hand on the last remaining SAS officer's shoulder. He squeezed and said, "He did you and your mates proud."

Jenkins nodded and said, "I know. Now let's go find the bastard responsible for this."

32.

Salvatori thought that he had lost track of time or miscalculated as the flash of light filled his vision. But somehow he was still alive. A tremor of pain lanced through his wounded side as he swiveled toward the explosion and wondered what had just happened.

As he watched the giant mushroom cloud billow skyward, he realized that the soldiers being used as a field test must have found a way to kill Cho's beast. He laughed, sending more tendrils of pain through his abdomen.

He checked his watch. Forty minutes until everything was set right again.

He looked back toward the mushroom cloud. He felt a stabbing of sadness that those soldiers had come so far and fought so hard. But now, despite all that, they would share his fate and be destroyed when the nuclear warhead contained somewhere deep below his feet detonated. He wished there was a way to warn them, but unfortunately, it was in God's hands now.

33.

After hot-wiring an abandoned Toyota min-van and picking up the kids, Knight drove toward a section of the city that, according to Jenkins, thermal scans from a British spy satellite had identified as giving off an unusual amount of energy. The area stood out like a flashing neon sign within a city that contained virtually no activity. Now that the beast was out of their way, they needed to track down its handlers, uncover their plans, and put them out of commission.

Unfortunately, the satellite photos could only narrow the search grid down to a radius of five city blocks, which meant they had a lot of distance to cover, and Knight feared that their prey would soon go to ground now that their little pet had been destroyed.

"This is it," Beck said from the passenger seat.

He slowed the van and began searching for anything out of the ordinary. The research headquarters could be housed within one of the surrounding buildings, but it could also be located beneath the city streets. He planned to make a couple of passes through the search zone and hopefully find some clue. If not, they would have to start a methodical search of every building, which could prove to be a dangerous and time-consuming prospect.

Up ahead, he caught sight of an old man sitting on the curb staring off into the distance. He brought the van to a halt and scanned the surrounding area for a trap. The interior lights of the van suddenly came on and the door ajar light flashed to life on the dashboard as Beck threw open the passenger door and ran toward the old man.

"Beck! Wait!" he screamed after her. He jerked open his own door and scanned the nearby windows with the FS2000. There were a million places to hide a shooter.

"Salvatori!" Beck called out as she ran.

The old man turned toward the sound of her voice and struggled to his feet. He stumbled back and nearly fell. Beck reached him just in time and steadied him. "Knight," she called over her shoulder.

He swore under his breath. He looked into the vehicle at Jenkins and said, "Keep an eye on the kids."

When he reached them, Beck said, "Knight, this is Dr. Giuseppe Salvatori."

He immediately noticed the man's gaunt features, shabby appearance and what appeared to be a bullet wound in his side. Those things spoke volumes to Knight and gave instant credence to the fact that Salvatori had been an unwilling participant in the events surrounding the creature's development. The old man extended his hand, and Knight took it. "Pleasure to meet you, doc. Pardon for me being blunt, but it's been a long day, so do you want to tell us what the hell is going on around here?"

Salvatori smiled. "At my age, Mr. Knight, you learn to appreciate the effectiveness of being direct. The creature that you've undoubtedly become quite familiar with, was the product of experiments conducted by a man named Phillip Cho."

"I remember Cho," Beck said. "He always struck me as a bit of a moron. Manifold security even caught him trying to sneak drugs into one of the facilities. I don't know how he managed to keep his job after that."

Salvatori bobbed his head in agreement. "Cho was a bit of a reptile himself, but he always had a way of surviving. I should have never gotten mixed up with him, but after Manifold was essentially shut down, I hated to think of how close I had come to making a significant mark upon the world. Cho gave me an opportunity to continue my work. He filled my head with lies, and by the time I learned his true plans, it was too late. He had used the resources of a splinter of the Chinese government, who hoped to prove the feasibility of world-wide communist domination to the government majority, to further his own insane scheme to achieve immortality."

"You referred to him in the past tense. What happened to Cho?" Knight said.

Salvatori laughed then winced and clutched his side. "Like the angel Lucifer, Cho's own vanity and pride were his downfall. Cho thought he had found a way to limit the side effects of his serum, but his manipulations to our original formula had actually caused additional side effects. He tested it on himself, and it killed him."

Salvatori looked to the horizon, but then his eyes suddenly shot back to Beck. With surprising speed, he reached out and grabbed her arm. The sudden movement made Knight's hand fly to his weapon.

"My God, Beck, in the excitement, I nearly forgot," Salvatori said. "We have to get out of here. I activated the facility's self-destruct system. In a few moments, the entire city will be leveled. Quickly, we must get to the roof. Cho has a helicopter up there, but I had no idea how to use it."

"Don't worry. I can fly anything," Beck said.

Knight's head jerked back to Jenkins and the kids. "Come on! We've gotta go now!" Jenkins ushered the kids from the vehicle and joined the others.

Salvatori turned toward the entrance to the building at his back, but Knight reached out and grabbed his arm. "Are you sure that Cho is dead and all of the research will be destroyed?"

Salvatori smiled. "Cho was paranoid. The only copies of the Hydra DNA and his research are contained here. No backups. And the changes he made to the serum surely killed him." But then Salvatori's eyes went distant for a moment. Knight waited, letting the doctor work through his thoughts. "Unless…"

The ground shook beneath his feet, and Knight said, "Is that from the self-destruct system?"

"No, it wouldn't be causing any tremors. Besides, we have—"

The ground shook with increased violence, and they struggled to stay on their feet. A giant fissure cracked open in the middle of the street in front of them, and the pavement bulged upward.

"What the—"

The street exploded. Pieces of pavement rained down around them. A thick cloud of dust filled the air and obscured visibility. Knight grabbed for the children, pulling them back from the gaping hole in the Earth and the falling debris.

A giant roaring sound emanated from the dust cloud. It was so loud that it shook his eardrums, and his hands instinctively flew to the sides of his head.

As the dust settled, he saw the giant creature climbing from a hole that Knight assumed to have once been a subterranean research facility. The enormous monster was misshapen and disfigured. It was humanoid in basic form and shared some similar characteristics with the creature they had just destroyed. It was vaguely reptilian and had elongated front limbs.

But unlike the previous creature, this monster was forty feet tall. Its skin pulsed and bubbled, and its body was disproportioned. Its bulbous elongated head bulged at odd intervals with strange tumor-like nodules. It reminded Knight of some nightmarish cross between the Hydra, a burn victim and the Elephant Man.

The grotesque abomination didn't seem to notice them. It stared at its hands and rubbed them over its malformed skull. It roared with one part agony and one part anger.

Jenkins, apparently struck with blind panic at the sight of the monstrosity, screamed and opened fire on the giant.

The bullet strikes had no effect other than causing the repulsive face to swivel downward and take notice of them. The massive creature that had once been Phillip Cho bellowed another deep roar. Then, as if smacking a bothersome insect, it slammed a giant misshapen fist down upon the final SAS survivor, grinding him into the pavement.

34.

Knight's training kicked in immediately, causing him to formulate a plan and act upon it while the others stood frozen in terror. "Beck!" She turned to him, her eyes wide and frightened. "Get to the chopper! Get the kids and the old man out of here. I'll buy you some time."

Once again, she didn't question his orders and instantly shoved the others toward the building's entrance. The giant's eyes followed the movement.

Knight took off toward the mini-van. He screamed at the top of his lungs and opened fire on the beast. The massive head jerked toward him and a clawed hand fell from the sky.

He dived forward and rolled as the street behind him was obliterated. The creature raised its hand to its face and seemed confused to not see a bloody smear.

Knight reached the van and swung the door closed. The accelerator slammed to the floor, and the van jumped forward with the sound of squealing rubber.

The beast swiped down and clawed fissures into the pavement, barely missing the van. Knight sped away down the street, dodging debris. The monstrosity bellowed and took off after him in an awkward, loping gate.

Knight skidded around the corner and saw one of the van's hubcaps rolling away in the passenger mirror. He took another immediate sharp left turn, trying to lose the creature.

The speedometer showed his speed increasing down the abandoned street. One eye remained on the rearview, expecting to see the giant appear behind him.

But then, he detected movement in a building coming up on his left. At first, he didn't know what to make of it, but then he slammed the brakes to the floor.

The building came toppling over into the street. Glass, concrete and steel girders exploded everywhere as he twisted the wheel to the side. The giant rode the crumbling structure to the ground. Knight whipped the vehicle around in the opposite direction and punched the accelerator.

He watched the monster gain its feet in the rearview. Then, he jerked the wheel away as a massive arm slammed down into the street at his side.

He kept the gas pedal to the floor as he swerved from one side of the road to the other. The van bounced up and down and nearly tipped over as he launched over debris from the shattering road. The beast continued to slam its fists down around him.

His heart slammed against his rib cage, and he felt like passing out from exhaustion. His eardrums vibrated from the beast's shrieking, and every muscle ached from fighting to maintain control of the vehicle amid the constant barrage of attacks and ground tremors. But he needed to keep the creature distracted long enough for the others to escape. He would have plenty of time to rest in a few minutes when the bomb went off.

The giant was right on top of him, stomping, slamming its arms down and trying to grind him into the concrete. Knowing that he couldn't keep this up much longer, Knight whipped the mini-van down an alleyway.

The opening was too narrow for the beast, but that didn't

stop the thing from slamming its formidable bulk into the adjacent buildings and trying to squeeze through. It shrieked in rage and rammed a clawed fist into the opening. But Knight was just out of reach. The creature slammed into the buildings again, and a large chunk of the brick building on Knight's left broke free and dropped into his path.

Caught between a rock and a giant reptilian monster, he goosed the engine of the mini-van and drove up the pile of debris as if it were a ramp. The van shot into the air and slammed against the building on the right, tearing off the passenger side mirror and sending out a fountain of sparks, before slamming back to the ground.

He glanced in the rearview, but the beast was gone. He didn't like the implications at all.

The alley grew dark as a massive shadow passed overhead. He stuck his head out of the window and looked up. The shadow continued forward, and he realized that the creature must have figured out that if it couldn't go through these buildings, then it could go over. Knight slammed on the brakes.

With monkey-like agility, the creature dropped to the ground in front of him and roared, blocking his exit from the alley.

35.

Knight could try to back up, but the creature would only come at him again from that direction. He had little choice. He stared straight into the beast's bloodshot, red eyes and then pounded his foot down on the accelerator. The van rocketed forward, momentarily startling the creature. It reared back from the opening, and the van shot onto the street.

The monstrosity recovered quickly, however. Its arm shot down and caught hold of the back of the van.

Knight gunned the engine one last time, but it wasn't enough to break the creature's grasp.

It lifted the entire van from the ground. Knight's breath caught in his throat, but his arms shot to the ceiling to brace himself. The world turned upside down as the creature spun the van in its enormous hands. It turned the vehicle over and over like a child studying a new toy.

Then it brought one of its reptilian eyes up to the window and shrieked again. The sound rattled the glass of the van and made Knight's ears ring. He could smell the stench of the beast's breath and the heat from its gaping mouth. The fangs inside the giant opening jutted out at odd angles, running down its throat and crossing over each other in a tangled mess.

Knight closed his eyes and braced himself for death with the knowledge that at least he had bought enough time for Beck and the kids to escape. Plus, the monstrous creature would be dead within a few minutes anyway.

He had accomplished his mission. His last mission.

But then he felt his stomach shoot into his throat as the van flew into open air. A blank white billboard loomed ahead, and the van smashed through it and flipped back over in the process. Before he could realize what was happening, the van struck the ground and skidded to a halt in the middle of a construction site. It grooved a long channel into the dirt, but the van finally came to rest.

Knight pulled his pistol and put a bullet into the airbags holding him in place. He thanked God and the patron saint of auto-designers for all of the modern crash safety features built into automobiles these days.

As he dragged himself from the wreckage, he felt a terrible pain in his side. It was difficult to breath. His head throbbed and blood was running into his eyes. He suspected that he had cracked ribs and either a broken nose or a fractured skull. He smelled gas and knew that he'd have a lot more injuries to contend with if he didn't get out the vehicle immediately.

He stumbled away from the van just as the creature's arm slammed down on it, compacting the mini-van into scrap metal. The impact shook the ground and jarred his bones. He toppled forward into the red dirt of the construction site.

Years of intense training were all that kept him moving forward, and he pushed himself to his feet and toward the skeletal frame of the skyscraper being constructed on the site. The creature apparently hadn't seen him yet, since he could hear it continuing to pound the van at his back.

He looked up at the frame of the building. It was only about six stories tall so far, and the top level held a large crane with a steel I-beam hanging suspended from its arm. He could see an open cage elevator sitting at ground level ahead and limped toward it.

He pushed through the belly of the building, past small concrete mixers and palettes of various building materials. The lift was only a few feet ahead.

The ground shook again, and the urge to look back overwhelmed him. But he fought down the impulse and pressed forward. He rushed into the lift, pulled the cage down and slammed the button to raise the elevator.

His breathing was shallow and labored. He wiped the blood from his eyes and fought to clear his vision. Dizziness and nausea swept over him.

Then, as he reached what he guessed was the structure's third level, a giant clawed hand clamped over the elevator's caged surface and blocked out the sun.

36.

Knight closed his eyes and prepared to be crushed. The lift's motor whined against the pressure and fought to pull the cage upward out of the creature's grasp. Smoke rose from the cables and the winch. The smell of burning rust was thick in the air. The cage around him began to buckle inward.

But then another sound drew his attention. He opened his eyes just as the creature pulled its hand away. He looked through the top of the cage as a chopper buzzed by the monster's head. The beast roared and swiped at the helicopter.

With the sound of grinding metal, the lift began to move again. Within a moment's time, Knight had reached the top floor. He stepped out onto a small wooden platform, but it only covered an area of about twenty feet. The rest of the floor was nothing but naked girders and sharp falls. The crane sat against the far opposite edge of the building.

He forced himself to breathe as he stepped out onto the girder. He felt like a tightrope walker in the circus, only he was performing without a net. With every step, breathing became more difficult, and he wondered if one of the broken ribs had pierced his lung.

The beast continued to howl below, and he could hear the

chopper buzzing by. But he tried to maintain his focus on not falling to his death.

Out of the corner of his eye, he saw the creature leap into the air and swipe at the circling chopper. He realized what was coming and tried to brace himself, but he wasn't quick enough. The beast came hurtling back down to earth. As it hit, the entire structure swayed and shook.

Knight lost his balance and tumbled over the girder's edge.

37.

Knight reached out and caught the edge of the girder. The downward force tore against his shoulder, and he felt like he had been stabbed in the chest as his broken rib grated against his internal organs. His breath left him, and his vision grew dark. He fought to keep hold of the girder, his only lifeline.

He reached down somewhere deep inside and found the strength he needed to hold on. He had survived terrorists, rebels, regenerating zombies, Neanderthal hunters, billionaires with god complexes, golems, giant insects, mutated reptiles and mythological beasts, and he would be damned if he was going to allow this big, ugly thing to be the death of him.

Tapping his last reserves of strength, he pulled himself back onto the girder and crawled forward.

After a moment, he reached the metal steps leading up to the crane's cabin. He pulled himself up and climbed inside. He quickly surveyed the controls and started up the machine. The buttons and labels were all in Chinese. Thankfully, he could read as well as speak most Asian languages.

He looked down and saw the gruesome creature swiping at the chopper. He knew that he would only get one shot at this, and the beast would need to be in just the right position.

With a pull of levers, the crane's arm swung away from the creature. Then he lowered the steel I-beam and put just enough slack in the wire to line up his shot.

The new movement drew the monstrosity's attention, and it swung toward him.

It was now or never.

Knight jerked the crane's controls, and the arm twisted toward the beast. The giant girder, being heavier than the arm, stayed in place for a second longer, but then the wire went taught and pulled the I-beam toward the creature. The momentum and weight of the large, red girder carried it forward like a missile.

It slammed into the beast's stomach and drove it back against the skeletal frame of the building. It roared in agony as the girder impaled it through the abdomen.

38.

A high-pitched wail emanated from deep in the creature's throat, but it didn't seem to have the same force behind it as its previous vocalizations. Knight suspected that the girder had pierced at least one of its lungs. The beast clawed at its own chest and fell to the ground.

Knight dived from the crane's cabin as the monster's formidable girth bent the metal supports and tore the crane free from the building. The remnants of the crane fell down on top of the creature. It clawed ineffectually at the girder and the debris of the crane. Knight wondered if the first creature's tenacity had been a result of it being created from a soldier who was accustomed to fighting and enduring pain while this abomination had been birthed from the body of a lab rat who probably cried for mommy after receiving a paper cut.

He heard the beating of rotor blades and looked up to the see the chopper descending on his position. He knew the Sikorsky S-92 transport chopper to be a solid craft capable of holding their whole group with room to spare. Beck sat behind the controls. The door in the side of the chopper fell open, and Salvatori dropped a rope ladder.

Beck maneuvered the rope into position, and Knight

reached out and grabbed hold. He felt like he hadn't slept in days, his muscles burned with every movement, and he could barely breathe. Despite all this, he forced himself to climb. Within a few seconds, he reached the cabin, and Salvatori helped him inside. Beck turned to him from the pilot's seat and gave him a wide grin.

But her expression quickly faded as the chopper lurched downward and she fought against the controls to keep them in the air.

He looked over the edge and saw the malformed face of the creature staring up at them. The girder was still lodged in its midsection, but it had somehow pulled itself up and grasped hold of the rope ladder. One good jerk of the ladder would tear them from the sky. He didn't have time to think; he only had time to react.

"Salvatori!" he screamed over the rotor wash. "Grab my legs!"

He didn't wait for the old man to respond. He simply slid the folding knife from his pocket, flicked the blade into place and flopped the top half of his body backward out of the open cabin.

He felt himself slide downward, but then Salvatori's weight fell on his legs. Another example of his small stature saving his life. A larger man would have dragged the doctor right out of the cabin with them.

His left hand reached for the rope ladder while his right readied the knife. With a sawing motion, the blade sliced into the rope. He looked down to see the gaping maw of creature full of crooked fangs. It tugged the rope toward it with a hand over hand motion.

His blade fought against the rope, but the ladder was military grade and must have possessed a high tensile strength.

"Hurry! We have less than two minutes before this whole city is destroyed!" Salvatori called down from above.

Knight wondered if Salvatori felt that he needed just a little more pressure. He tried to ignore the old man, the countdown and the beast below and focused upon the rope.

With a final motion, the last stubborn strands peeled apart, and the chopper jerked upward, nearly causing him to tumble out.

But Salvatori held firm, and Knight pulled himself back into the cabin. Beck didn't waste any time as she pushed the chopper away from the city at full speed. The children stared back at the empty buildings as if in shock. He opened his arms wide, and they leapt on top of him. He pulled them in tight against his body and covered their heads with his hands.

Salvatori counted the seconds down aloud. "Five...Four...Three..."

The sky behind them went completely white. It was as if God had decided to wipe the canvas clean and start fresh. Then reds and yellows burst into existence on the blank canvas. Finally, he could see the outline of the mushroom cloud.

"Hold on!" Beck screamed.

The shockwave crashed into the chopper along with a terrible burning odor. Knight closed his eyes and held tight to the children. The S-92 twisted and spun like a roller coaster ride. Salvatori gasped, and the children sobbed into Knight's chest. It felt as if the vibrations were tearing him apart from the inside out.

Then it was over. And they were clear of the blast.

Knight gazed back toward the mushroom cloud and the ruined city for a few moments. The children continued to cling tightly to his body. He gestured with his head for Salvatori to come over. The old man hobbled across the cabin, sat down next to Knight, and took hold of the children. They didn't say a word as he passed them off. They merely gravitated to Salvatori as they did him. Any port in a storm, Knight supposed.

He walked to the front of the chopper and joined Beck in

the cockpit. He slid into the co-pilot's chair and slipped on a headset. She looked over at him. "I owe you one," he said.

"Damn right, you do. I saved your ass back there."

He laughed. "I'd say that's about right."

"So I assume you remember our wager," she said.

He looked confused for a moment, but then his smile fell. "If you think that you're getting me in a bikini, you're out of your damn mind."

EPILOGUE

Knight took his cell phone away from his ear, switched it off and put it in his pocket. His conversation with Deep Blue had been surprising to put it mildly.

He pushed his feet beneath the hot sand until his toes reached the cool, wet sand below. He'd returned to Thailand with three days left on his reservation. His suit had been ruined beyond repair, but he had packed for weeks. Of course, the shorts and T-shirt he wore now cost less than one hundred dollars—beach fashion for men was essentially identical, whether you spent fifty dollars or a thousand. On the beach, it's the body beneath the clothes that matter.

Not that beach bodies were on his mind. His current company managed to keep his eyes from straying too far in any other direction.

"You know, standing in the sand like that just makes you look shorter." Beck said as she stepped up next to Knight and handed him a cold beer. She'd worn the bikini after all, and she wore it well. "Who were you talking to?"

"My boss," Knight replied. "He had a few interesting things to say about you."

"Your boss?"

Knight nodded and tried not to smile when he saw her tense.

Despite himself, Knight's thoughts about Beck weren't just physical. He'd fought alongside the woman. He respected her. And he enjoyed her company. He rarely found all three qualities in a woman he also found so attractive and had told himself to take this slowly.

Ling and Jiao, who Salvatori had taken on as his responsibility as penance for his collusion with Cho, had revealed a desire for a more profound relationship. He wasn't remotely ready to consider children or a wife. But a girlfriend?

He watched Beck's face purse up as she wondered what Knight's boss had said about her and he enjoyed every expression. *Yeah*, he thought, *I could make that work.* But he didn't want to rush it. And if Deep Blue had his way, Knight would have plenty of time to make things work.

"Yeah," he said. "My boss. Here is what I'm authorized to tell you. Your knowledge of certain Manifold facilities, your exceptional record, your experience with security, your current "off the grid" status and having proven yourself to me—the team—twice, makes you uniquely qualified for a job."

"A job? You're hiring mercs now?"

"Actually, we can, but not you. Deep Blue, my boss, was wondering if you'd like to head up Chess Team's internal security. It would be a full-time position. In the States. No running. No hiding."

Beck turned toward the smooth blue ocean, lost in thought, her expression unreadable. When Knight could no longer take the silence he said, "Personally, I hope you turn him down. I don't know if I could stand to see you so often."

Beck smiled and turned to him. "Well, if it would annoy you, I'm in."

Knight couldn't hide how much her answer pleased him.

A new kind of silence passed between them. It ended when Beck cleared her throat. "You know, for a Spec Ops killer, you're kind of a chicken shit."

"What?" Knight said, taken aback.

"You can kiss me now."

Knight froze in place for just a moment and then thought, *screw taking it slow*. He pulled his feet out of the sand, stood on the tips of his toes and kissed her. Almost dying had never seemed so worthwhile.

ABOUT THE AUTHORS

JEREMY ROBINSON is the author of numerous novels including PULSE, INSTINCT, and THRESHOLD the first three books in his exciting Jack Sigler series, which is also the focus of and expanding series of co-authored novellas deemed the Chesspocalypse. Robinson also known as the #1 Amazon.com horror writer, Jeremy Bishop, author of THE SENTINEL and the controversial novel, TORMENT. His novels have been translated into ten languages. He lives in New Hampshire with his wife and three children.

ETHAN CROSS is the International Bestselling Author of The Cage and The Shepherd–a book that has been described as "Silence of the Lambs meets The Bourne Identity" and "A fast paced, all too real thriller with a villain right out of James Patterson and Criminal Minds."–and the pen name of a thriller author living and writing in Illinois with his wife, two daughters, and two Shih Tzus.

ALSO IN 2011

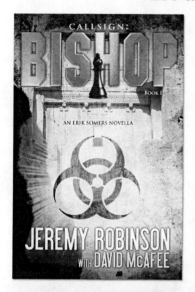

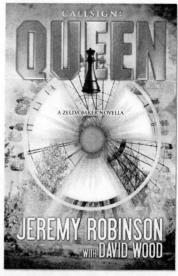

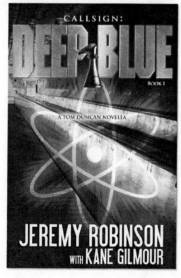

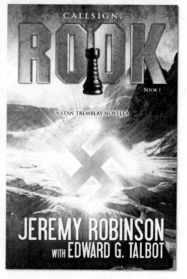

CPSIA information can be obtained at www.ICGtesting.com
Printed in the USA
LVOW090943270612

287868LV00003B/7/P